2099

revolution

John Peel

BOOK 4

AN
APPLE
PAPERBACK

SCHOLASTIC INC.
New York Toronto London Auckland Sydney
Mexico City New Delhi Hong Kong

No part of this publication may be reproduced in whole or in part, or stored in a retrieval system or transmitted in any form or by any means, electronic, mechanical, photocopying, recording, or otherwise, without written permission of the publisher. For information regarding permission, write to Scholastic Inc., Attention: Permissions Department, 555 Broadway, New York, NY 10012.

ISBN 0-439-06033-8

12 11 10 9 8 7 6 5 4 3 2   0 1 2 3 4 5 6/0

Printed in the U.S.A.

First Scholastic printing, March 2000

*This is for Debbie and Kevin McCormack
and Shannon, Erin, and Brendan.*

2099

revolution

Prologue

There was nothing quite like being master of your own world. Right now, Devon was only ruling the Moon. But it was a start — good practice for when he took over Earth. Start small, and work your way up. . . .

Devon was in his base of operations, an old NewsNet studio he'd taken over and modified to fit his needs. One wall of the main room was filled with Screens. These had images from all over the Moon on them; since he'd taken over LunarNet, he could watch anything the security Monitors detected. It was a shame the Monitors couldn't see inside people's homes, like on Earth. Devon had become quite addicted to watching how normal, boring people ran their dull little lives. For one thing, it made him so much more grateful for his own brilliant, exceptional life.

All he could do here was watch the corridors and public areas that made up the bulk of Armstrong City. Still, that was plenty.

Like the small group of six shields trying to sneak in and capture or kill him without being spotted. They'd been smart enough to disable the Monitors in the tunnel they were using so he couldn't actually *see* them. They were dumb enough to think that this was enough. It made him chuckle to himself, that they would think he was as stupid as they were, and wouldn't realize that something was wrong.

As soon as the Monitors had died, he'd suspected trouble, and he simply used the other, nonvisual, sensors to confirm it. Since he controlled the air supply on the Moon, nobody could breathe without his permission and attention. The sensors indicated that six people were in the blanked-off corridor, breathing quite heavily. The heat-scanners then picked up the tazers that the shields carried, since tazers had a unique heat scan. Devon rolled his eyes. *Puh-lease!* They might as well have been wearing signs saying WE'RE TRYING TO SNEAK UP ON YOU.

"Well, time for stupidity to gain its just reward," he

decided. With a smile, he cut the power to the corridor. Immediately, doors descended, sealing both ends. By now, the shields would know they'd been rumbled, and they'd be getting worried. Good. And since they'd left *him* in the dark, it seemed like a nice idea to return the compliment. He killed the lights. Finally, since they were all breathing heavily, it seemed like the best way to punish them was to remove all the air from the corridor. After all, they were only breathing because *he* was nice enough to allow it. If they weren't appreciative of his kindness, he'd revoke their privileges.

He started to drain the air from the corridor.

The sensors showed lots of frenzied movement. The shields were no doubt trying to find some way out of his little trap. Unfortunately for them, there wasn't one. Their tazers couldn't burn through the metal bulkheads in time — and if they tried, the heat-beams would use up what little air was left. The shields were already gasping for breath. And there was no way out through the walls, which were solid Moon rock overlaid with wiring and other conduits.

They would pay for trying to be nasty to him.

His Terminal showed that all of the air had gone from the corridor. There were no signs of breathing any longer. He played with his panel for a few minutes, and finally managed to get the Monitor looking out at the corridor again. The six shields had all collapsed, their faces red and twisted in death.

Served them right.

Humming to himself, Devon switched to look into the governor's office. Well, technically, the ex-governor's office, since Devon was now really running things. The politician was a stout man, nervous, with a tendency to sweat when things went badly. He was sweating now, which made Devon chuckle.

"Your little attack didn't work," Devon informed him, and enjoyed watching the man squirm. Devon switched the picture to show the dead shields. "You can't get at me," he said patiently. "And look what you made me do. I *really* don't want to have to kill any more shields, so please restrain yourself from trying silly little tricks like this again, okay? I'm in charge, and I'm going to *stay* in charge. I'll let you off this time. I'd have been very disappointed if you hadn't tried *something*. But next time, I'll have to punish you as well. Okay?"

"You *killed* those men," the governor protested weakly. He was sweating heavily.

"No," Devon said patiently. "*You* killed them, by sending them to hurt me. I can't allow that. So don't do it again, okay? Oh, I'm opening up the doors now, so you can go in and get them out and bury them somewhere. They make that corridor look *so* untidy." He

4

switched over the Screen, not wanting to hear any more of the idiot's whining. How could he ever have gotten to be governor in the first place? The man was such a wimp and a loser. And now he'd lost everything — to Devon.

It was fun being in command. Devon rubbed his hands together and studied his favorite Screen shot. It was a view across the outside of Armstrong City, looking up into the sky, which was always black here on the Moon. The rising Earth was a searchlight in the darkness. He could see the blue of the oceans, and the wisps of white clouds. Then there were the familiar continents, stretched across the fragile globe.

Earth would be his next conquest, as soon as he'd had enough practice running the Moon to be able to take it over properly. He stroked the Screen, enjoying the view. Soon, very, very soon . . .

1

Taki Shimoda sat in her office in Computer Control, wishing she could scream and break something. Until a few days ago, she'd been plain Inspector Shimoda of the shields, and she had almost enjoyed that — at least until the appearance of a mysterious computer hacker who had almost destroyed New York City with his Doomsday Virus. She had managed to track down the madman, a teenager named Tristan Connor, and she'd arrested him. He'd been tried and sentenced to Ice — the top security prison in the Antarctic, where the most dangerous prisoners were sent. That *should* have been the end of her problems.

Instead, it had barely scratched the surface. In her hunt for Tristan, she'd been helped by a young girl named Genia, who had lived in the Underworld. Shimoda had never been there, beneath New York where the outcasts were thrown and forgotten, but Genia had grown up down there. The young girl had survived to become a slick computer thief, until she'd managed to obtain a sample of the virus. That had placed her life in danger from Quietus, the organization of unknowns behind Tristan's plans to destroy the Net. Shimoda had helped Genia, and had promised her protection. But she'd been unable to keep her promise. Shimoda's boss, Peter Chen, had ordered Genia arrested; then she too had been sentenced to Ice. Shimoda felt that she had let the girl down, and it was obvious that Genia felt exactly the same way.

But Chen's interference had shown Shimoda something very important — that there were traitors within the shields themselves, the very force that had sworn to protect the human race. Shimoda took her oath very seriously indeed. Now that individual nations existed pretty much in name only, the shields were their only defense against anarchy. All of the old national armies had been disbanded — with no outsiders to fight any longer, they were both unnecessary and foolishly expensive. Instead, the old police forces of the world's countries had joined together and formed the shields. The idea that a person could join the shields, promise to do their best to help people, and then turn traitor made Shimoda sick. But she had discovered so much evidence that Quietus had somehow managed to turn a number of shields into members of its own organization that she had to accept it.

The latest evidence was the worst. A group of thugs had invaded Ice and attempted to either free or kill Tristan Connor. Instead, somehow, Connor and Genia had joined forces and used Ice's own defenses to knock out the raiders and to escape themselves. That was bad enough, but Shimoda had only known about the attack and escape because Tristan had sent her a message about it. When a shield force investigated, they discovered that the raiders were shields themselves.

Those renegade agents were now imprisoned on Ice, but they left Shimoda with a lot of serious problems. First of all, she didn't know who to trust. Her boss, Peter Chen, had turned out to be a traitor working for Quietus, but she knew it was very unlikely that he was the only one. There had to be others in her department. She had her suspicions about Judge Montoya, for example, though she had no proof of the woman's guilt. That was the problem — she had plenty of suspicions, but no clear-cut answers. The only person she completely trusted was her old friend Jill Barnes. But the two of them couldn't do everything. She needed to have the captured shields on Ice interrogated, but she had to be sure that the people doing the questioning were on her side.

And she could think of only one way to do that.

"Miss Shimoda."

She glanced up and managed to smile as Martin Van Dreelen walked into her office. He was the vice president of Computer Control, which effectively made him the second most powerful person on Earth. He was also her only boss right now, and had appointed her to the post. She could only pray that he was on her side, and not using her for some elaborate game of his own. Her secretary, Tamra, had heard that other members of Computer Control were less than thrilled with her appointment, and Shimoda could understand that. She had, after all, virtually no real credentials to hold the job Van Dreelen had forced upon her. A lot of more senior people had been passed over. Van Dreelen had claimed it was because he could trust her and not them, but was he telling the truth?

That was the problem with suspicion — once you started suspecting people of treachery, it was awfully hard to stop.

"Mr. Van Dreelen," she replied, rising to her feet and

shaking his gloved hand. "I'm glad that you could spare me the time." She was rather amazed that he'd come in person, rather than just through a Virtual Reality projection.

"I'm sure it must be important," he answered with a slight smile. "And, besides, I thought I'd remind you that I was hoping we could have dinner together some evening."

"Dinner?" Shimoda remembered him asking her, but had assumed it was only polite conversation, and not a real invitation. "I wish I had the time to eat at all right now. There's just so many problems to solve first."

"I know what you mean." He sat down in a chair beside her desk, and gestured for her to do the same. "Maybe when your workload lets up a little? I have so few opportunities to simply enjoy myself, and I'd really like to get to know you a little better. But that has nothing to do with why you wanted to see me, I assume?"

"Hardly." She took a deep breath. "I want your permission to use Truzac on everyone in Computer Control. Specifically in the shield and justice divisions. We have too many potential turncoats in our midst, and I *have* to know who we can trust and who we can't."

"Truzac?" Van Dreelen looked slightly amused. "I'm not sure that would be a good idea."

"Why not?" Shimoda demanded. "Anyone under its

influence has to tell the truth, after all. We simply ask them if they're loyal to Computer Control or to Quietus. That will tell us all we need to know."

"There are two problems with that," he answered. "First, I've seen reports that claim Truzac isn't infallible. People can make themselves *believe* things that aren't true. And in that case, Truzac is useless. Plus, it may not work on everyone. There are suggestions that members of Quietus might have an antidote to the drug."

"But it would at least give us a chance," Shimoda insisted. "What you're saying is only *maybes*. Those reports could be wrong."

"Of course they could," Van Dreelen agreed. "But that's not the main problem. The main problem is that we can't simply insist that people *have* to take Truzac. People have rights, Miss Shimoda. And forcing them to take a truth test would break those rights. I can't allow you to do that, I'm afraid."

"But —"

"No." He shook his head firmly. "Believe me, I do understand and sympathize with your problem. I have it, too. But walking over the rights of people isn't the solution we're looking for here. Truzac can only be applied if the person is *accused* of a crime. Not simply suspected. And you aren't even suspecting people —

11

you're asking *everyone* to take it, just in case. It's impossible."

Shimoda felt deflated. This had been her only hope. She had to be *certain* she could trust the people she gave assignments to, and there was no other way to be sure. "Then we might as well not have the shields anymore," she said bitterly. "We can't *assume* they're working for us any longer."

"It's not that bad," Van Dreelen assured her. "Look, there can't be more than maybe one percent of the shields who really work for Quietus. That means that ninety-nine percent are honest and conscientious, and can be trusted."

"But it's that one percent that causes us problems. Until we can identify them, we're almost paralyzed."

"Then it seems to me that the thing to do is to find Quietus. They are bound to have a list of their agents. Once we have that, we'll know who we can trust." He stood up, forcing her to do the same. It was obvious that she'd get nowhere with him. He'd made his decision — a *political* one, not a practical one — and he clearly wasn't going to budge. "I have confidence in you, Miss Shimoda. You'll work it out." He paused in the doorway. "Don't forget about dinner," he reminded her. "Let me know when you can spare time."

He'd been gone only a minute when Tamra came into

Shimoda's office. The secretary was a nice young woman, and Shimoda only hoped she was right in trusting her. She had, after all, worked for Peter Chen before Shimoda. "He's no help, is he?" Tamra asked.

Shimoda scowled. "How did you know that?"

"Aside from the look on your face?" Tamra grinned. "Because I make a habit of listening in on what goes on in this room."

Shimoda could hardly believe the cheek of the woman! "You know you're not supposed to do that!" she exclaimed, embarrassed and angry.

Tamra shrugged. "It helps me do my job better if I know what's *really* happening, and not simply what my boss tells me." She bit at her lower lip. "Look, Taki, we've been friends for a while now. I'm pretty sure I can trust you, and I hope you feel the same way about me. Because I think you've made a *major* mistake."

"So do I," Shimoda answered. "Accepting this ridiculous job."

"No, seriously." Tamra moved in close and lowered her voice. "I think you've been conned. I don't think Peter Chen is a traitor at all. I think he was framed."

Shimoda hadn't been expecting that. "Tamra, I was the one who found most of the proof of his guilt."

"It was planted," Tamra insisted. "Look, I listened in on his office just as I do on yours. I know what he was doing. If he'd been a traitor, I'd have known. And I can assure you, he didn't do anything wrong."

"Sure he did," Shimoda insisted, confused and puzzled by Tamra. "For one thing, he was the only person who knew I was coming back from Overlook with Tristan Connor as my prisoner. And we were attacked. Only he knew where to find us."

"Not so," Tamra answered. "I knew, for one. I listened in when you talked to him. And I promise you, I didn't tell anyone else. But Peter did. He told Van Dreelen."

"Van Dreelen?" It was as if a cold hand had grabbed her heart.

"Yes."

Shimoda thought about this for a moment. "And when Tristan was free, Chen didn't put out an arrest-on-sight order. . . ." She had a suspicion she knew what was coming next.

Tamra tapped a code into Shimoda's Screen. "He did; but it was immediately overridden, as you can see."

The facts were there on the Terminal. And the only person who could have countermanded Chen's orders was someone of higher rank — like Van Dreelen. "I'm starting to see why he didn't want me to give people Truzac," Shimoda muttered. "He'd be the first to fail my loyalty test. But if all this is true" — she waved her hand at the Screen — "then Chen's innocent, and most likely Van Dreelen is our traitor."

"Exactly." Tamra looked grim. "What are we going to do about it?"

"I don't know yet," Shimoda answered. "But I promise you, I will know soon. We're going to get the real villains behind all of this, whatever happens." A sudden thought came to her: the most obvious person who could have gotten clone samples from Borden was another Computer Control member — which again pointed to Van Dreelen as the guilty person. And he could have told Chen about Genia being wanted, if he was a member of Quietus. It was all starting to fit together.

And it all meant that the conspiracy was worse than she had imagined . . .

2

Tristan was at a complete loss — and not for the first time in his recent memory. Every time he thought things were getting better, they'd somehow get worse. Having teamed up with Genia, he'd escaped from Ice — supposedly an impossible feat. And now, having successfully given every shield on the planet the slip, he found himself at tazerpoint again. Only this time his captor was the last person he'd have ever expected — his ex-girlfriend, Mora.

Worse — she seemed to be really enjoying this.

He glanced at Genia, who looked more annoyed and disgusted than scared. They were standing in Genia's apartment in the Underworld of New York, where he and she had hoped to get some food, rest, and equipment before going on with their quest to stop Devon and clear both their names. Instead, they'd walked right into a trap laid by Mora, of all people! She was a Mora he hardly seemed to know.

"Why are you doing this?" he asked her.

"Because you've ruined my life, Tristan Connor!" she exclaimed. "I had a really nice life until you messed it up. Now look at me! I've been sentenced to spend the rest of my life in the Underworld. My parents have lost everything. My friends must think I'm scum. And all because you've gone completely crazy." She glared at him. "I used to think I loved you, but now I know you're just filthy trash." Then she smiled. "So I'm going to make you pay for what you've done to me."

"Is she for real?" asked Genia scornfully. "I think she's been overdosing on soap vids. '*I'm going to make you pay for what you've done to me,*'" she mocked, and rolled her eyes. "Maybe you should look into getting a vid writer to come up with your next threats. Something original like *Today Genia's apartment — tomorrow the world*?"

"Don't try to be funny," Mora growled. She hefted the tazer in her fist. "Don't forget who's got the weapons around here. And the troops." She gestured at the heavyset men with her. "Right now, the only thing I've got against you, girl, is that you've latched on to my boyfriend. That shows monumental bad taste, but nothing worse."

Genia sighed very theatrically. "You just got through saying you don't want him anyway. And, besides, I'm not latched on to him or anything. We're just working together. I guarantee you, there have been no smoochy bits to our relationship. It's strictly business. I'm not interested in bonding with anyone."

Mora shrugged. "Maybe you're telling the truth and maybe you're not. I don't care. You're not the one I'm after." She glared at Tristan.

"Fine, then I'll just leave." Genia started to do so, but the tazer moved to cover her.

"I said *I* wasn't after you." Mora smiled brightly. "However, the man I work for wants you very badly. His name is Barker."

"Barker?" Genia went pale.

Tristan cleared his throat. "Much as I hate to interrupt you two, will somebody tell me what is going on here? Who's Barker?"

"He's the scum of the Earth," Genia answered. "If your girlfriend here's part of his gang, she's crazier than I thought. Barker has a vision of being the emperor of the Underworld. He's been getting himself a little army of thugs and morons." She gestured at the men standing by impassively. "They're the thugs; she's one of the morons."

"Watch that tongue of yours," Mora snapped. "Or I may be tempted to burn it off at the roots. Barker wants to question you, but I'm sure he'll be happy to do it with a speedboard instead of speech."

Genia looked at Tristan. "If she was always like this, I don't know what you ever saw in her."

Tristan was starting to wonder that himself. This wasn't like the Mora that he'd known and thought he loved. She'd been funny, happy, and great to be with. *This* girl was filled with anger and hatred. Maybe she'd always had this potential inside of her, and it had never come to light. He remembered that Marka, Mora's kid sister, had contemptuously called Mora a jerk. Maybe Marka knew more about her sister than Tristan had — until now.

But he couldn't just give up on her. "Mora," he said gently, "I know you've had a bad few days. So have I, believe me. But I'm not the one that caused your troubles. We're both victims of the same people. It's not me you want to hurt, but *them.* Join forces with us, and we can put things right."

Mora laughed. "Oh, suddenly you're a crusader for truth and justice?" she mocked. "The same Tristan

Connor who released a virus that destroyed New York? The same Tristan Connor who's being hunted by the shields?"

"I didn't create that virus," Tristan informed her. "It was my duplicate. *He's* the one behind all of this."

"Oh, right." She rolled her eyes. "Now who's been watching too many soap vids? Your evil twin is responsible for all of this? Tristan, you're an only child."

"Not exactly." Tristan felt sick because he could tell he wasn't getting through to her. "According to Devon, I'm his clone. I know cloning is illegal, but somebody's still doing it, and I'm part of the result. Look, it's *really* important that we stop Devon before he finishes off WorldNet next."

Mora glanced at Genia. "And *I'm* the one who needs better scripts for my stories?" she mocked. "Listen to that load of drivel."

"He's telling the truth," Genia insisted. "I know."

"Right." Mora shook her head, and then turned to the nearest thug. "I think it's time for the fun to begin. I'm getting bored listening to these two. Gag them both. Then tie Tristan to a chair over there. I think it's time for *him* to suffer for a change."

Tristan tried to protest, and he could see Genia tensing to fight. But with half a dozen huge hulks with tazers in the room, trying to escape was pointless and probably lethal. They were both held and gagged with magnetic tape. Tristan was then fastened with more magnetic tape to one of the chairs. Mora came over to him, smiling. She stroked his cheek with the cold metal of the tazer barrel.

"I've been learning a lot recently that I didn't know before," she informed him. "For example, do you know how tazers work on the human body? They send an electrical shock to the nerves. It feels like somebody's set fire to your skin, and then it knocks you out. But if you lower the intensity a bit, it doesn't knock you out. It just leaves the I'm-charred-toast feeling." She held up the tazer and let him watch her lower the setting a notch. "This just hurts like nothing you can imagine, or so I've been told." She smiled. "I'm kind of looking forward to finding out if that's the truth. It's payback time. . . ." She leveled the tazer at his stomach.

Tristan was sweating badly, and was more scared than he'd ever been. There was absolutely no doubt in his mind that Mora was going to do exactly what she'd just described. He was going to live in pain until he couldn't take it anymore. The thought terrified him, because he'd never been able to deal with pain without medication. And that *Mora*, of all people, should be the one doing this to him . . .

Her finger pressed down on the trigger button, and

there was a smile on her face and in her eyes. Whatever she had felt for him once was now long dead.

"That's enough," a gruff voice snapped.

Tristan, Mora, and Genia all looked around. Only Mora could speak, and she said what Tristan couldn't ask.

"Barker? What's wrong?"

Barker was a tall gray individual, and he had a certain air about him that told you he was dangerous. He strode into the room, accompanied by a woman and four more of the huge thugs. He glared at Mora, obviously annoyed, and also, it seemed to Tristan, disappointed. "I sent you here to get the secrets that this girl hid." He gestured at Genia, who muttered something unintelligible from behind her magnetic tape. "Not to torture your ex-boyfriend."

Mora shrugged. "So I'm adding pleasure to business; where's the harm in that?"

"There's no profit in it," Barker answered. "I thought you understood that profit is all we're interested in down here. No profit, no point."

"It'll profit *me*!" Mora exclaimed.

"Yes, but *you* work for *me* — and I get nothing out of a fried corpse." He walked over to Tristan and pulled the magnetic tape off his face. Tristan yelped, since Barker had made no effort to be gentle. "Can you offer

22

me a profit for keeping you alive? And pretty much unhurt?"

"I don't know," Tristan confessed. "It all depends on what you consider valuable. The world, maybe?"

Barker grinned. "Nice offer, but what would I do with the world? I couldn't possibly run it. I'm a modest man, and I know my limitations."

"That's not what I meant," Tristan answered. "I meant that I'm probably the only person who can keep the world from falling apart." Genia made some valiant attempts to protest. "Well, maybe the two of us," Tristan conceded.

Barker shrugged. "I don't much care what happens to the world," he admitted. "It's never done much for me. Why should I care what happens to it?"

"The way I understand it," Tristan said, desperately hoping he was right, "you rob the rich Above, right?" He had won over Genia by appealing to her greed; he doubted she was the only one this worked with.

"True enough, kid." Barker was starting to look bored.

"If Devon gets his way, there won't be any rich," Tristan explained. "There probably won't even be any Above. There won't be anyone for you to rob from, and nothing to steal. Devon wants the world to collapse into chaos. And where's the profit in that?"

Barker rubbed his chin. "You've got a point there," he admitted reluctantly.

"He's lying!" Mora growled. "There isn't any Devon! *He's* the one trying to destroy everything!"

"Why would I do that?" Tristan asked desperately. He *had* to convince Barker, or everything was lost.

"Why would Devon want to do it — if he exists?" asked Barker reasonably.

"Because he's convinced he's better than everyone else," Tristan answered. "He thinks he should be in charge. He wants to destroy everything."

"Sounds pretty dumb to me," the woman with Barker commented. "What's the point in destroying everything?"

"So he can gain control of what's left," Tristan said. He was actually guessing a lot of this, based on what he'd seen of Devon and figured out, but he didn't want them to know he was unsure. "So that he can convince the survivors that they *need* him to stay alive."

"You expect us to believe that?" Mora sneered. "Barker, he's lying!"

"Let Genia speak," Tristan urged, realizing he was losing here. "She's one of you; she has no reason to side with me if I'm lying, does she?"

"He's got a point, Barker," the woman said.

Barker nodded slowly. "Okay, Lili, take off her gag. Let's hear what she has to say."

The woman, Lili, walked over to Genia, and ripped off the magnetic tape. Genia yelped and then swore. "You could have been gentler!"

Lili shrugged. "So? You want to speak, or do you want the tape back?"

Glowering, Genia shook her head. "I'll talk. Listen to Tristan; he's telling the truth. There's this group, Quietus, that aims to take over the world, and Devon is the one they're using to make it happen. If they win, I guarantee you, we all lose."

Mora moved forward. "She's his girlfriend," she protested. "Of course she'll back up his story!"

"More than you ever did," Genia sneered. "*You* were supposed to be his girlfriend, weren't you? What turned you into psycho-girl? Losing your nice clothes and missing a meal?"

Furious, Mora backhanded Genia, leaving a trail of blood from the other girl's mouth. Genia moved her jaw, which obviously hurt. "Well," she said, spitting blood, "I'd say that's not a very convincing argument."

"Can you top it?" Barker asked.

"Sure." Genia grinned. "Computer, code alpha blue."

There was the sudden sound of locks engaging.

Barker and his men looked around. Tristan didn't know what was happening, but he was almost certain Genia knew what she was doing.

Almost.

"What's going on?" Barker demanded, moving closer to Genia.

"I've had about as much of this as I'm going to take," she replied smugly. "I've just set the self-destruct mechanism on this apartment. You've got two minutes to set me free, or it all goes up."

Mora laughed incredulously. "A *self-destruct*?" she sneered. "Talk about watching too many soap vids!"

Genia managed somehow to shrug her shoulders. "Suit yourself. If I'm going to die anyway, I always figured I'd take my killers with me. I hate going anywhere alone, even into the afterlife."

"She's bluffing," Lili said. But there was sweat on her forehead, and Tristan could hear the uncertainty in her voice.

"Genia," Tristan said urgently, "don't do this! I'm sure I can convince them! If we die, then nobody can stop Devon!"

"I don't much care," Genia answered. "You may be Mr. Idealist, kid, but I'm not. If I die, the world can die, too, as far as I'm concerned. I don't care about the world, because it doesn't care about me." She smiled quite contentedly at Tristan. "And don't even think about trying to get out of here; you can't override my computer."

Mora was looking very scared. "We can make her talk!" she growled, hefting her tazer. "This will hurt her so badly, she'll stop the computer!"

"I'm sure it will," Genia agreed cheerfully. "I don't think I could hold out for more than an hour. Of course, you've got less than a minute, so it won't help."

Tristan stared at her, sweating himself. He didn't like the idea of dying, and especially not while there was the threat of Devon. But he could see that Genia was being stubborn. There was no doubt in his mind that she would do what she had promised. She'd sooner take everyone with her than die alone. He looked at Barker. "She's not bluffing!" he said. "Let us go! We have to help one another now, not attack one another."

"You think I'm afraid to die?" Barker asked, his eyes filled with annoyance.

"There's no profit in it!" Tristan yelled.

Barker considered the point, and then finally nodded. "Okay. I'll listen to you. Now, turn that bomb off."

"Say please?" Genia suggested.

"Do it!" Mora screamed.

Genia sighed. "Computer, pause zero one nine."

"Affirmative."

The girl glanced at Barker. "That's put a short halt on the countdown, nothing more. Now set us free and we can talk. I'll cancel the detonation when we reach an agreement." She grinned. "So if you were thinking of killing me when I stopped the bomb, you're out of luck."

To Tristan's surprise, Barker grinned back at her. "Now I know why you always managed to keep one step ahead of my men. Even if we don't agree on what to do next, you and that other kid won't die. I give you my word on that. I like your nerve, girl." He laughed. "But I can't say I won't rob you blind."

"Fair enough." Genia seemed happy with the compromise. She glanced at Tristan. "Whatever else Barker is, he's no liar. We can trust him — to do *exactly* what he says, and nothing more."

Lili produced a knife and sliced through Genia's bonds. Then she did the same for Tristan. The woman gave him a curious look. "It seems like we might end up on the same side, after all. It's a strange world, isn't it?"

"Believe me," Tristan said, "I'm only just realizing *how* strange." Here he was, teamed with crooks, on the run from the shields, accused of crimes he hadn't committed, and being stalked by his ex-girlfriend. Could the world get any stranger? He stood up, rubbing his skin where the rope had burned him.

Genia brushed against him and whispered, "Thanks for backing my bluff."

Bluff? Tristan was sweating now; Genia had been lying all along in order to keep them alive. . . . Wonderful. Now he had to try and convince Barker to join forces. . . .

3

Jame was having serious problems, and, for once, staring out of the windows at the red sands of Mars didn't help. In the past, he'd always been able to relax and forget his troubles when he'd sat in front of one of the large view windows and looked out at Syrtis Major. The red sands and pinkish sky were normally so soothing. But not today.

His whole life was being wrenched apart, and he didn't know why. He had discovered that the people he'd always believed to be his parents had actually adopted him as a child. They had never mentioned this to him, and it had only been almost by accident that he'd found out the truth. What he was going to make of it, he didn't know. He still loved his parents, but he was feeling insecure.

A good part of that was due to the Administrator having declared martial law. Armed shields now had the run of the community, and they had started a reign of terror by gunning down workers who had only been looking for their jobs back. Jame had witnessed the killings, which the Administrator claimed were meant to stop an attempt at a revolution. Jame knew this was not true, but even his own father didn't believe him.

Jame still loved his parents very much. Even if they weren't biologically related, he felt an emotional attachment to them both that was stronger than blood. But they *had* disappointed him. Why hadn't they entrusted him with the truth? And why did his father find it so hard to believe him?

It was no good; he couldn't sit around while the Mars he loved went to pieces. Jame didn't care what anyone else did; *he* couldn't just stay out of this. The Administrator was wrong, and if his parents sided with that tyrant, then they were wrong, too. The only person who seemed to have kept his head right now was Captain Montrose. He was in charge of the original shield forces, the ones here before the Adminstrator had brought in the "reinforcements" from Earth. The newcomers were the ones killing the residents of Mars, not Montrose's men. Jame knew he had to go and join the captain and help stand up for what he believed in.

He was under no illusions: he knew he was putting his life in danger. Since the Administrator was in charge of Mars, disobeying his commands was treason. And, right now, the Administrator was punishing treason by death. But as much as Jame wanted to live, he wanted to be able to live with himself. If he faltered now, how could he ever do that? He knew he owed his parents an explanation first. And maybe, just maybe, this time they'd listen to him.

They were together in their virtual office, which was hardly surprising. They had a lot of work to do, considering the fact that the colony was working under a state of emergency right now. Jame hesitated for a moment, but he decided that what he had to say was more important right now than anything they were doing — since whatever they were doing was to help the Administrator. Jame had, long ago, played all through their Terminal, and he'd set some bugs, more for fun than for actual use. Now was the time to use them.

He killed their link to the Administrator's Monitors, and then closed down any links that might help the Administrator listen in on what was happening here.

Maybe he was just being paranoid, thinking that the Administrator would care about one unhappy teen. But a bit of paranoia might be what he needed to keep him alive.

Both of his parents sat up from their VR helmets with a jerk as they lost their feed. Jame shrugged, a little red-faced. "Sorry about that," he said. "But it's really important that you both listen to me right now."

His father looked shocked, and then annoyed. "I don't know what you've done, Jame," he snapped, "but Mars is in the middle of a crisis right now, and I have important work to do. Restore my link immediately."

"Sorry, Dad," Jame answered. "No can do. You're working for the wrong side."

"How can you say that?" his mother asked sharply. "You can't possibly mean that you're siding with the *rebels*! They're out to destroy the colony!"

"No, they're not," Jame insisted. "Look, I've tried to talk to you before, and you wouldn't listen. This time you have to, if you want me to uplink you again." He tapped his wrist-comp. "I can do it, but only if you hear me out."

"Jame," his father growled, "do as you're told. This is not the time —"

"This *is* the time," Jame said firmly. He refused to

back down now. "The Administrator is the one doing all of this. There were no rebels until he started killing unarmed people. He's crazy, and you should be trying to stop him, not working for him."

"Jame," his father said, trying to sound reasonable, "you don't know what you're saying. The Administrator is a good man. He works for Quietus, too, and we all want to help people."

"Like you helped me?" Jame asked. "By adopting me when Quietus ordered you to?" He raised an eyebrow. "Were you ever going to tell me that?"

His mother sighed. "Is that what this is about?" she asked sympathetically. "You discovered that you're adopted, and it's upset you?"

"No, Mom," Jame said. "You just don't get it, do you? Yes, I'm kind of mad you never told me, but that's not the point here. That's just a minor problem."

"We never told you because we never thought much about it," his father said. "We always thought of you as our son, and I guess we simply didn't think it was necessary to tell you that you were adopted. But if it bothers you —"

"*Listen* to me!" Jame interrupted. "It bothers me, but I can cope, okay? That's not the real problem here. The problem is that you're working for a psycho! Here." He tapped the commands on his wrist-comp, and the

Screen on the wall lit up. "Watch this. It's the security camera that recorded the first part of the *rebellion*."

His mother sighed again. "All right, dear, if it makes you happy." They both turned to watch.

This was the original version, before the Administrator had managed to add in some fake scenes of people with tazers in the crowd his shields had shot to pieces. Only one of the striking workers had a tazer, and he was shot down before he could use it. The rest, unarmed, were simply slaughtered. Even though he'd seen the event itself while he was hiding, and then watched this vid again since, it still hurt Jame to watch people being killed for no real reason.

It served to shut his parents up and to get their attention, though. They watched the recording in stunned silence. When it was done, Jame switched off the Screen. "The Administrator . . . adjusted the record," he told them. "Check the timing on that vid if you don't believe me, and then look at the one the Administrator's been giving out. You'll see his is forty seconds too long — because of the fake footage he inserted. He's lied to you, he's lied to the people here, and he ordered those shields from Earth to kill people."

"But *why*?" his mother asked. Her face was ashen, and she was clutching his father's arm. "Why would he do such a thing?"

"I was kind of hoping you could answer that," Jame said. "I don't know. Except that the one worker who tried to shoot the shields yelled that it was for Quietus. If he was telling the truth, and if the Administrator also works for Quietus, I'd say that you've both been lied to about what their real aims are."

His father stumbled, trying for words that obviously wouldn't come. Finally, he managed to find his voice. "That *can't* be true!"

Jame sighed. "Dad, it *is* true. Live with it. The Administrator and Quietus have been playing you both for idiots. You're idealists, and they lied to you to make you believe in them. But now that you know the truth, what are you going to do about it?"

His father's face set grimly. "I'm going to speak to that monster!"

His mother gasped. "Charle, you can't be serious!"

"I have to," Mr. Wilson insisted. He turned to Jame. "I know you're better with the computers than you've ever let on. Can you access the Terminal in the Administrator's office?"

Jame nodded. "Sure. That's how I got the *real* vid footage."

"Then monitor it while I speak to the man." His father looked grim. "Right now, what we need to know is what he's planning. And the only way we can do that is if I confront him and demand the truth. The old blowhard loves the sound of his own voice, and I just know he'll tell me what's going on."

"I'm sure he will," Jame's mother said. "But what will he do *after* that? He's not going to let you go. You'd be too dangerous."

"He'll probably throw me in jail." He shrugged. "But I'm not much use for any fighting, anyway. Lise, I want you to take Fai and Jame and go somewhere safe. There's going to be a lot of trouble."

"Dad" — Jame's voice caught — "this is probably not a good idea."

"Well, then I'll be batting a thousand," his father replied. "I've made a lot of bad decisions in my time. But adopting you was not one of them." Briefly, he hugged Jame. "Look after your mother and sister."

"I will," Jame promised. He felt as though his father was going off to die. The Administrator was crazy, but surely he wasn't *that* crazy? Jame realized that they had no way to tell. His father released him, kissed his mother, and then left the domicile. Jame expected his mom to fall to pieces crying, but instead she simply looked determined.

"Get that link up, and record whatever happens," she ordered him. "Can you patch it from here into your wrist-comp? I'm sure that as soon as your father speaks to the tyrant, he'll send some shields down to arrest us."

"No problem," he assured her, already working on it.

"Good. I'll get your sister. Be ready to leave in five minutes." She paused. "Do you have any idea where we can hide?"

"With Captain Montrose," he suggested. "He's got some real shields, and is holding out against the new ones."

His mother thought about that for a second, and then nodded. "Get onto it." She vanished to get his infant sister.

Jame worked fast, setting up what they needed, and then grabbing whatever tools he might need. There was no telling how long or how vicious the fighting might be. He had to be prepared for anything. He was ready inside the promised five minutes, and had a pack slung over his shoulder when his mom returned with Fai and another pack of baby supplies.

"Let's go," she said, her voice hard. Jame knew she had to be as scared for his father as he was, but she wasn't showing anything but anger and determination. As they left their domicile, his link flashed.

"Dad's there," he said.

"Put it on audio," she suggested. "We can listen as

we go." He did as she asked, and they hurried along, their ears straining to hear what was being said.

"You lied to me, Administrator," his father's voice snapped. "I've seen the original vid of that so-called rebellion you put down. Those shields from Earth shot down unarmed men and women."

Jame had expected the Administrator to lie, but he'd underestimated the madness of the man. He could almost see the shrug. "I did what I had to, Charle," the Administrator said glibly. "It's very important at this moment that I take firm control of the seven cities of Mars. I can see that you're upset, but —"

"Upset?" his father yelled. "You *killed* Martian citizens without warning or cause. You *bet* I'm upset! What the devil do you think you're doing here? People are *dying* because of you."

"I'm well aware of that," the Administrator answered. "And I'm truly sorry that it has to be done." He didn't sound anything but smug. "Quietus needs Mars to be under our control. The time is almost here for our arising."

"What garbage are you talking?" his father demanded. "What arising?"

The Administrator's voice became firm. "Quietus. But I can see that you're not in a rational mood right now,

Charle. I understand, and I empathize with your pain. But I can see that you have forgotten that you pledged to help Quietus achieve all of its aims. Right now, I clearly can't trust you to follow through where you are needed."

"I agreed to help Quietus because I genuinely thought it stood for good," his father said bitterly. "I can see that I was very foolish to believe that."

"No, you weren't," the Administrator answered. "I know things look bad at this moment. But they will get better. Charle, the end of the world is upon us, and only the strong will survive. *We* are the strong, and we must *stay* strong. You'll understand soon that what I'm doing really is for the best. But until then, I'm afraid that I'll have to put you somewhere where you can't do yourself or others any harm."

"Tell them to let go of me!" his father yelled. Obviously a couple of shields were arresting him. Jame felt rather relieved; he'd actually been terrified that the Administrator would simply shoot his father as well.

"I'm sorry, Charle," the Administrator replied, his voice oily. "Not until you understand what is happening. Take him away. Then send a squad to his domicile and bring his family in as well. It might . . . help if he realizes what could happen to them."

Jame's face flushed. The Administrator wanted to

hold them hostage for his father's behavior! It was a good thing Dad had realized that might happen, and had them leave. Jame turned off the sound, but continued to record. Having a link into the Administrator's office might be a lifesaver soon. He looked at his mother, and suddenly realized what a strong woman she was. She had to be terrified for Dad and for them, too, but nothing showed on her face except resolve. She caught his anxious look and smiled grimly.

"Don't worry," she vowed. "He's going to pay for everything he's done. I promise you that, Jame. *Everything.*"

Despite his fears, Jame felt a little better. He was sure his mom meant everything she said. And he'd hate to be anyone who stood in her way right now . . .

Together, they hurried down the corridors. With his computer bugs, he'd get them past the patrolling shields and into safety with Captain Montrose.

But then what would they do?

4

The Malefactor sat at his Terminal, tapping his fingers, fuming. Just as Quietus was on the verge of achieving all its long-term goals, it seemed as if things were determined to fall apart. Their main thrust for power had finally begun — after almost thirty years of waiting! And now . . . problem after problem. Some of them would undoubtedly be blamed on him.

Devon, principally. The young computer genius had, in one way, worked out wonderfully. The boy had been everything that Quietus had needed — brilliant, skillful, and without the cumbersome baggage of morality that so many people carried around. Armed with these weapons, Devon had created the Doomsday Virus. It was capable of entering, and then destroying, every computer in the world, and of ravaging the underlying computer Net that linked the human race on Earth together.

The problem was that those same talents had led Devon into making serious mistakes. He'd unleashed the virus in a test, which hadn't been agreed to by Quietus, but had alerted the authorities to trouble. The Malefactor wasn't too worried about Computer Control, though. It was supposed to be in charge of all computer activity in the world, but it was a complacent, slow-moving bureaucracy. On top of that, Quietus had already infiltrated it, and it was — even though it didn't know this — already under Quietus's control. The problems lay elsewhere.

First of all, with the shields. The stupid police force had lucked out a few times, and they didn't seem to know when to quit. Quietus had a lot of agents in the shields, of course, but not enough. And most of those were needed for the main plan, especially since several of the agents had been captured in the botched raid on Ice and in the attempts to capture or kill Tristan Connor. Quietus still had dozens of agents as shields, but there were over a hundred thousand genuine shield agents out there. And one in particular was causing trouble: Taki Shimoda.

The Malefactor had favored simply killing her, but his attempt failed. The Controller had preferred to move the woman to a different post, and that had now been accomplished. She'd been promoted from her investigative job to a desk job as head of Net Security. The Controller thought this would keep her out of their way, unable to work against them and tied up in bureaucratic red tape. The Malefactor wasn't so sure; the woman was proving to be a more formidable foe than they had originally expected. He'd still sooner see her dead, but had been overridden. The Synod of Quietus would soon realize their mistake.

His *real* headache was Tristan Connor. He'd planned carefully to have the boy captured or killed, and had come close several times. Only each time, the youth had somehow escaped — he'd even managed to get out of Ice, which was supposedly impossible. Now he had vanished. The Malefactor was certain this wouldn't be for long; the boy would be back, a thorn in his side. And, to top it all off, Devon had vanished.

The Malefactor took another dose of tranks for his headache, and thought things through. His priorities right now were clear: recover both boys. While his agents were searching for signs of both of them, though, there was another task to finish. He had to find out just who Tristan Connor was.

When Quietus had bred Devon, they had created a backup clone of him, in case the boy should prove hard to handle — as in fact he had. The clone was hidden, and ready to be activated at any time. The Malefactor had originally thought Connor was that clone and had managed to get free and create havoc. But according to the Administrator, Jame Wilson was still on Mars. And if Wilson *was* on Mars — then who was Tristan Connor?

There was only one possible answer — one that the Malefactor had been dreading and avoiding. If it was true, then Quietus had bigger problems than he had ever imagined. He triggered his projection software, and his real form was cloaked in the dark shapeless-ness that everyone outside this room of his saw as the Malefactor. Only two people in all the world knew his real identity, and he intended to keep it that way.

He sent the message, and a moment later the simu-lation of his target formed around him, thanks to his holographic projectors.

He seemed to be standing inside the Zero Project anteroom. There were no windows, of course, and the walls were of buffed metal, reflecting images dimly. Be-hind the single desk in the room sat Dr. Tedescu, the project head. He was completely bald, with thick glasses, through which he blinked at the image of the Malefactor. Since all eye problems could be surgically and genetically corrected, the Malefactor knew that the glasses were fakes, used to intimidate the unwary; they didn't intimidate him.

"Malefactor," Tedescu said, trying to look delighted. "To what do I owe the pleasure of this visit?"

"Stupidity," the Malefactor answered. "Or carelessness. And I mean yours and not mine. Take your pick. Either way, I'm here to get information."

Tedescu blinked. "I'm afraid I don't understand," he said. The Malefactor could see that the doctor was thinking fast, trying to anticipate what had gone wrong.

"I'm also afraid you don't understand," the Malefactor agreed. "That's the problem. Now, I want you to open the Doomsday Project Area. We will go in together, you and I, and check it out."

Tedescu blinked furiously. "But that area has been sealed since the two clones were removed fourteen years ago," he protested. "By order of the Synod —"

"By *my* order, we're opening it," the Malefactor growled. "You don't want the Synod to know what I believe has happened yet. Move."

Tedescu was a brilliant geneticist, but a weak human being. As the Malefactor had known he would, the man caved in. "Very well," he agreed. He moved to the door, and the Malefactor seemed to walk with him. They entered a short corridor, which led to several doors, and went through one. Another corridor led to three sealed doors. Tedescu approached the left-hand one, and placed his hand into the niche.

"Computer," he ordered. "Unseal the Project Area."

"Scanning," the Terminal replied as it checked his voice and DNA sample. After a moment, it said, "The Project Area has been unsealed."

"Understood," Tedescu answered. "On my authorization, open it."

"Affirmative."

With a sigh, the door unlocked. Then the six-inch steel door slid open on immense rams, straining because of disuse. As soon as he could, the doctor stepped inside, and shivered. He glanced at the image of the Malefactor with some envy. "It's cold in here," he complained.

"Then don't waste time," the Malefactor snapped. "Check the clone bins."

The room was small, only four feet deep and about ten feet long. It held nothing but monitoring equipment and twelve upright flasks, each some two feet high and wreathed in ice. Atop each flask was a monitor, blinking red.

Tedescu approached the first flask and used the edge of his sleeve to rub at the monitor, clearing off the thin frosty layer. "This was the flask that contained the first clone," he reported. "It is empty, naturally."

"Devon," the Malefactor said, nodding. "Continue."

The doctor moved to the second flask and repeated his wiping gesture. "The second clone. Empty also."

"Jame Wilson," the Malefactor agreed. "Continue."

Tedescu moved on. "The third flask," he reported. "Stable. The fetus is still in cryogenic suspension and viable." He glanced up at the Malefactor. "There is no problem with this?"

"None. Continue."

Tedescu moved on. Flasks four, five, and six also held viable clones of the Devon basic. All were in suspension, waiting the chance to be brought to life. The first problem was flask seven. This had no status markers, and Tedescu peered at it in confusion. "There is no readout."

"I can see that, you idiot," the Malefactor growled. "Why is there no readout?"

Tedescu checked the control panel, and tapped in an inquiry. "A short in the mechanism," he reported. "Power appears to have died in this flask."

"Open it."

"But . . . it has been without power for months, possibly years . . ."

"OPEN IT!"

Tedescu nodded hastily, and worked at the covering. After a few moments of straining, he managed to get it loose. Then he staggered back, reeling. "The stench!" he complained, coughing. "The fetus is dead."

The Malefactor was glad the simulation he was in didn't include the sense of smell. "Close it then, you fool. As long as the fetus is there, I don't care if it's alive or dead."

Hastily, Tedescu obeyed. The Malefactor could hear the whine of air purifiers cleansing the room, and Tedescu finally looked a little more comfortable.

"Continue," the Malefactor ordered implacably. The doctor didn't dare disobey, even though he obviously didn't want a repeat of flask seven. Eight and nine were fine, but ten made the doctor pause again.

"This one is empty," he reported slowly. "The fetus has been removed."

The Malefactor cursed. It was what he had been expecting, after all, but not what he had wanted to hear. "Can you determine *when* this was done?" he demanded.

Tedescu checked the computer logs. "Two weeks

after the removal of the first two clones," he finally said.

"And I doubt there's any indication of who might have opened the flask?" the Malefactor growled.

"None," Tedescu confirmed. "Whoever it was covered his or her tracks well. The code used is . . . mine." He looked up, alarmed. "But, I assure you, I did not —"

"I'm sure you didn't." The Malefactor was telling the truth; Tedescu was far too weak to be able to commit such treason and then face up to him afterward. "Your codes and DNA were no doubt stolen and used while the Devon and Jame clones were being brought on-line."

"But . . . that means . . ." the doctor gasped, struggling to understand.

"That someone within Quietus removed the third clone and brought it on-line themselves," the Malefactor finished. "The third clone has also grown up; his name is Tristan Connor, and he is also working against us. Whoever removed the clone is a traitor to Quietus, and is also working against us." He sighed. "I doubt it will do much good, but go through the records. I want to know the names of everyone who was physically present in the Project Area on the day the third clone was removed. *Everyone.* Then we shall start checking to see which of them could have stolen it." He glared at the doctor. "I know it will take some work, but this is of the utmost priority. We *have* to find out who the traitor in our midst is, and eliminate him or her."

"I understand." Tedescu nodded nervously.

"Now," the Malefactor ordered, "check the remaining flasks. We've already got one unwanted clone running around. I'd hate to discover that there are more."

Tedescu moved fast. "The others are still locked and viable," he reported.

"Good. Now, seal the area again. I want those vaults under constant surveillance. If anyone tries to get near them, inform me immediately."

"Of course." The doctor swallowed nervously. "Er . . . What are you going to tell the Synod?"

The Malefactor knew the doctor was scared; this botch-up was, after all, his responsibility. There was no need to reassure the man, even though he was too valuable to terminate. Let him worry; it might make him belatedly more efficient.

"It depends on the results of your search," the Malefactor replied. "If we can use this to isolate and identify our traitor, you might still be considered a useful worker. If not . . ." He let the threat dangle and severed the connection.

Sitting back in his chair, the Malefactor sweated. He was in a very bad position right now. Though he had discovered who Tristan Connor was, the answer made Quietus's problems worse. There was a highly placed traitor in their midst, and he didn't have a clue as to who it might be. Until he found out, he didn't know which of his fellow Synod members he could trust.

The irony wasn't lost on him: Shimoda was having her problems attacking Quietus, because she didn't know which of her shields were loyal. Now he, too, was having problems for precisely the same reason. He'd never imagined he'd ever have anything in common with a shield, and yet now he had.

It felt terrible.

5

Zenia was feeling quite happy with herself, now that all of the arguing was over. Tristan was a nice kid, which was probably his problem — he was *too* nice. He didn't understand the realities of the world. He'd grown up sheltered and pampered, with a lovely little family in a lovely little house with a lovely little girlfriend. And then that world had collapsed about his ears, and he still hadn't learned to adapt. He was lucky to have her around to show him how things *really* worked.

On the other hand, it must have been nice having a life like that, instead of the one she'd had. Sure, it had made her tough and adaptable, but the thought of actually knowing you didn't have to fight for your next meal — or anything else you needed — was very tempting. Even if it did make you kind of soft. . . . Genia sighed. It seemed like you couldn't win, either way.

Still, Tristan didn't do so badly. He'd managed to convince Barker to give him a chance, and that was a lot more than Genia had expected him to do. Of course, he'd had her help, like with the bluff about the self-destruct program. (Some people would believe *anything*!)

She watched Barker and Tristan hammering out the final details of Tristan's plan, as she worked on her own part of the plot. Thankfully, she'd been building a spare of her ImplantChip duplicator just before the troubles had started, and it wasn't taking much work to finish it off. She'd never had an IC, and Tristan had been forced to remove his own. Mora's had been neutralized when she was sent to the Underworld.

Speaking of whom . . . Genia saw that Mora was glaring at her again. Mora was the only one not happy with the new alliance. She had a scowl on her face as dark as a storm cloud. Genia didn't care. She didn't much like the girl, and was amazed that Tristan had ever found her attractive. Well, okay — Mora had short golden hair, and a kind of nice face, if that's what you liked. Not like Genia's long dark hair and brooding face.

"What are you looking at?" Mora demanded sullenly.

"The biggest idiot I've ever met," Genia replied pleasantly.

"Are you looking for a fight?"

Genia laughed at this. "Girl," she answered, "don't start trouble with me. I could whip you ten ways from Sunday. Even if you had that tazer. You're not as tough as you think — and I am."

Mora glared at her, but wisely didn't dispute the fact. Instead, she changed the subject slightly. "I suppose you think you're hot stuff, don't you? Stealing my boyfriend?"

Genia sighed and rolled her eyes. "You've got a one-circuit mind, haven't you? Well, it's so small, there's not enough space in there for a second. First of all, I don't date *anyone*, much less Tristan. Second, I didn't *steal* him, you threw him away. Third, you'd better decide if you want him dead or just want him. And fourth, he's too young for me."

Mora glowered at her. "You'd better get your own tiny little mind straight. If you're not interested in him, what difference does his age make?"

Genia found herself flushing, without quite knowing

why. Probably just because the other girl was so irritating. She bent back to her work. "Why don't you go stick your finger in a power socket?" she suggested sweetly. "You're no use to anyone here."

Mora snarled wordlessly and went away. Genia finished her work, and went to join Tristan and Barker with her device strapped to her arm, under her voluminous sleeve. "All set," she reported.

"We're almost ready," Barker said, eyeing her device. "Nice piece of work. It feels kind of funny working with the two of you — but also kind of interesting."

"What are we waiting for?" Genia asked.

"Lili to return," Tristan said. "It turns out that she was a doctor before she was sentenced to the Underworld. She's got a supply of Truzac we can use, and knows how to give it."

"Sounds good," Genia agreed. "Though I think Mora was kind of hoping to get to use the tazer to torture the information we need out of the judge."

Tristan looked a little hurt at her comment, but didn't say anything as the door opened and Lili and the two men sent to look after her returned. She had a small bag slung over her shoulder.

"Ready for action," she said. "I haven't got much Truzac, I'm afraid, so you'll only get one chance to ask questions."

"One chance is all we should need," Tristan said confidently.

"Don't be so sure," Lili warned him. "Truzac isn't a magic wand, you know. It only makes people tell the truth — not *all* the truth, mind you, just a direct answer to whatever you ask them. They won't volunteer anything, and if they can avoid revealing anything, they will. You have to be very careful what questions you ask."

Tristan nodded. "I understand."

"Good." Barker rubbed his hands together. "Let's get going, then. I have to confess, I'm rather looking forward to whatever the two of you come up with next. At least life isn't dull around you and Genia."

They moved out of her apartment, and Genia reset the traps. Now that there was power restored to the city above them, her defenses were working properly again. Nobody else would be able to break in the way that Mora had managed.

The group of them headed back toward the waterfront, where the hovercraft Genia and Tristan had used to escape from Ice was hidden. On the way, a low howl echoed through the streets. Barker's men tightened their grips on their tazers, and Mora looked scared.

"What's that?" she asked.

"The Tabat," Genia answered, shivering. "It's out hunting again."

"What's a Tabat?" asked Tristan.

"A mythical beast that hunts and eats people," Barker answered.

"Not so mythical," Genia assured him. "It killed a couple of thugs from Quietus and accidentally saved my life." She shuddered. "I'd rather not have to thank it. I don't think I'd survive a second encounter."

"It might be a good time to hurry, then," Lili suggested. She didn't need to say it twice; they all moved a little faster.

The hovercraft was where they had left it, hidden in a broken-down building on the waterfront. Nobody had tried to tamper with it, which was hardly surprising, since it was an assault ship and Tristan had programmed the defense mode. He switched this off, and the party entered the craft. Genia slid into the pilot's seat, since she had worked out the controls the last time they'd used the vessel, and powered it up as the rest strapped themselves in. Barker sat in the cabin with her and Tristan, but the others stayed in the passenger area.

"You know where we're going, I hope?" Barker asked.

Tristan patted the nav-comp. "I have a small worm in the mainframe at Computer Control," he said. "I used it to dig up Judge Montoya's address."

Barker whistled. "There must be *some* way I can get

the two of you to work for me." He was almost begging. "Why, you're the two most natural thieves I've seen in my life."

"Thanks, I think," Tristan answered. "But I'm normally very law-abiding, and I intend to return to that lifestyle once I've cleared my name."

"That's a crying shame," Barker sighed. Then he looked hopefully at Genia. "How about you, kid?"

"I'm independent," she replied proudly. "I don't need help to be a thief. And I don't see why I should share what I know with anyone. At least, not once this is over."

"That's the trouble with youth today," Barker complained. "No ambition."

Tristan chuckled, and plugged in the route they'd take. Montoya lived in a large house in Toms River, in New Jersey. That was on the coast, so they could travel a good part of the way there in the hovercraft. Then they'd have to continue on foot, since the shields would probably be looking for the vehicle. That was when things would get interesting.

As it turned out, though, there were fewer problems than Genia had anticipated. They stowed the hovercraft and left two of Barker's men with it. The rest of them went on into the town. Like most towns, there were few people out by day, but they needed to get to one of them. Finally, Genia saw the perfect target — a man out jogging.

"Tristan, with me," she said. "The rest of you, stay out of sight till he's gone. He's going to be suspicious otherwise. Nobody travels in groups these days."

They did as they were told, and Genia grabbed Tristan's hand. "Pretend we're out for a bonding stroll," she told him. "He'll think we're strange, but nothing more." She liked the idea of making Mora jealous; it served the stupid girl right. She cozied up to Tristan, almost rubbing against him. He seemed a little uncomfortable but went along with it. Genia pretended to be fascinated by Tristan's ear, leaning into it while actually watching the jogger get closer. "Now, say something in my ear," she whispered. Tristan did so.

Immediately, she jerked free and gave him a stinging slap across the face. "What kind of a girl do you think I am?" she yelled, and was amused to see his face turn bright crimson — and not just from the slap, either. She whipped around as if to run away from him, and, as she'd planned, slammed "accidentally" into the jogger.

He oofed in pain and lost breath. She grabbed his hand to steady him. "Sorry!" she gasped. "It's just that this idiot . . ." Her IC scanner read his implant, and her ring nipped his skin, taking a small sample of his DNA.

"None of my business," the jogger said, trying not to

look at her. He pulled his hand free and hurried off, finding his pace again. Genia grinned at his back: Perfect! He'd been so embarrassed at seeing a "lover's quarrel" that he hadn't even realized she'd stolen his identity.

"Maybe next time you'd warn me what you're going to do?" suggested Tristan, rubbing his red cheek.

"And spoil that wonderful natural reaction of yours?" she asked, innocently.

As soon as the man vanished around the next bend, the rest of their gang hurried out of hiding to join them. Mora looked furious, which amused Genia considerably.

"I got what we need," Genia reported. "Come on."

They hurried on to the judge's house. This was the only part of the game that was educated guesswork. The same judge, Montoya, had tried and sentenced her, Tristan, and Mora. Maybe it was coincidence, but Genia didn't believe it; the judge had twisted the law in each case, rather than obey it. To her mind, the woman *had* to be working for the opposition.

The judge's house was large and set back from the road. It had a well-tended garden, which was interesting, though not unusual. No doubt the judge could afford a gardener; as long as he wasn't around now. . . .

He wasn't. And Tristan had already determined via

his hand-comp that the judge was at home, since it was the weekend. Did she have any other workers in the house who might get in the way? There was no way to tell just yet. There was a metal security fence around the house, but that didn't bother Genia too much. She'd broken through worse. Using the stolen IC information and the jogger's DNA skin sample, she accessed the "visitor" program in the gate's Terminal. Tristan used this to hack into the security codes, and overrode them. Genia had to admire his skill at this; if she was honest, she knew he was better at some things than she was, and this was one of them.

The gate opened without alerting the judge to the fact that she had visitors. Quietly, they all moved up the pathway to the house. Genia and Tristan repeated their act, and the front door opened.

Now it was Barker's turn to take the lead. He listened for a moment, and then gestured forward the two thugs remaining with him. They nodded and moved off. Barker looked bored as they all waited inside the first room they found. A moment later, the two men returned, half dragging, half carrying Judge Montoya between them. The woman looked both indignant and scared.

"What do you think you're doing?" she was yelling as Genia stepped forward.

"Hi," Genia said cheerily. "Remember me?"

The judge stopped struggling for a second as she stared at Genia until recognition dawned. Her eyes opened wide, and then refocused as Mora moved forward, her tazer held ready.

"And me?"

Tristan completed the shock by joining them. "Three's a charm," he said.

"I was only doing my duty . . ." the judge began.

Genia shook her head. "Oh, I don't think so," she replied. She gestured at a nearby chair, and the thugs slammed the woman into it and held her there. "I think you were actually setting us up to be killed by Quietus. And we're going to find out if that's true or not."

Lili moved forward, a dermal sprayer in her hand. "Truzac," she informed the judge. "It won't hurt you, but it will make you . . . cooperate."

"You're lucky," Mora added, tapping the woman's cheek with her tazer. "I wanted to do it the hard way. The old-fashioned way. The see-how-much-screaming-they-can-do way. But I was voted down." She smiled, not at all pleasantly. "I rather hope the Truzac doesn't work. I'd love to prove my friends wrong."

This didn't make the judge feel any better, obviously. She struggled, but there was no point to it; Barker's thugs held her too tightly, and Lili gave her the spray.

"Now," Lili said cheerfully, "it's time to sing, little bird."

6

Tristan watched as Judge Montoya struggled and then went limp. One of the side effects of Truzac was that it calmed people down, so he'd been expecting this. Lili examined the judge quickly, and then nodded. "She's under the effects now. It'll last maybe half an hour, depending on how much she fights it. I don't have enough for a second dose."

"Hopefully, we won't need it," Tristan answered. He moved to stare at the judge. She seemed like a nice, middle-aged woman, but that *had* to be just a front for what she really was — otherwise he and Genia were sunk. He started the recording mechanism on his hand-comp. "Who do you work for?" he asked her.

"Computer Control," she replied without hesitation. "I'm a judge." Tristan felt his stomach plunge; he was horribly afraid he'd made a mistake.

Genia growled in her throat. "Get with it, Tristan. She's fighting the drug by telling the exact truth. You have to ask better questions than that." She turned to the judge. "Are you a member of Quietus?"

"Yes."

Tristan was relieved, and a little embarrassed. Genia was right, he had to be more careful. "Why did you join Quietus?" he asked. He had to get some preliminary information, so he'd know what to ask later.

"Because I believe in its aims," the judge answered.

"And what are they?" Tristan wanted to know; they were his enemies, and he didn't really know why.

"To rebuild the human race," the judge said. She seemed quite happy, and elaborated for the first time on her answer. "About thirty years ago, the founders of Quietus saw that the human race was going wrong. People were too dependent on computers, on their machines, on their comforts. They were getting soft, flabby, out of shape, both physically and mentally. They had stopped being *alive*. Machines and especially computers were really doing all the work and thinking. Quietus saw this, and understood that it had to change. But it was a long-term project. The founders started the program, and recruited those of us who were smart enough to see the truth, and dedicated enough to be willing to work to change things. The vast majority of the human race is soft, idle, and complacent. They just want to be fed and amused. Quietus saw that this had to be changed."

"By force?" asked Tristan. There was something oddly believable about the aims of Quietus. He could see that; but he could see also that the organization was doing illegal things to force their views on everyone.

"By whatever means are necessary. Persuasion, if possible. Force, if people won't listen. To change the world, you have to take *action*." The judge seemed very eager to explain. "The only people really living were those on the frontiers. That was when Mars and the Moon were starting to be colonized. They were the true human race, not the fat, lazy cows who stayed on Earth and just took what they could get. Quietus wants to improve the species, and that was our model."

"*Your* view of what the human race should be," Barker said. He looked annoyed.

"Of course," the judge replied. "Only the superior

mind and superior body should live. Letting *anyone* contribute to the human race is self-destructive. Look at the animal kingdom — the weak and the unfit die, so that the race will be strong."

"Human beings aren't animals," Lili pointed out forcefully. "No matter how badly we are treated."

The judge looked at her without concern. "*You* are," she said calmly. "Everyone in the Underworld is just scum on the pond of life. You should all die and improve the species."

Mora growled low in her throat and raised her tazer. "And you condemned *me* to be a part of that?"

Tristan slapped her hand down. "Knock it off, Mora," he ordered. "Listen to her, don't argue. We know she's a fanatic, if she's part of Quietus. But we have to find out what's happening, not waste time trying to make her see sense." He turned back to the judge. "Is that why you started the cloning project? To try and improve the human race? Is that what Devon is — your idea of Superman?"

"Yes. The Zero Project was the Malefactor's responsibility. The idea was not merely to clone a human being — that's been possible for almost a century now, even if the process was forbidden by law. The idea was to *alter* the species, to make it better."

Tristan felt a chill. "Then I'm not just the clone of

some person?" That would explain why he'd been able to find no close relatives when he'd checked his own DNA on the WorldNet. . . .

"No. The Malefactor took various samples of human DNA and had his scientific workers put them together. They designed the genes of this person to be a brilliant computer programmer. The idea was that he'd be the first of a better, improved version of the human race. One without weaknesses."

"Without morals," Genia said bitterly. She glanced at Tristan, and then seemed to realize something. "Wait a minute — *you're* his clone!"

"And just as bad as him?" Tristan asked. The same thought had occurred to him. If Devon had been bred to be without scruples, to simply be a genius — then that made Tristan just as bad at heart.

"No, that's not what I mean," Genia said. "*You* have morals — too many, if you ask me. So Devon isn't quite what they thought, if you can think for yourself and not be exactly like him."

"Am I Devon's clone?" Triston asked the judge.

"No," she replied.

Tristan stared at her in shock. Was the Truzac working? Could he believe her? "He said I was his clone — is he really *my* clone?"

"There were twelve of you created," the judge explained, "but only two brought to full life. You have identical DNA, but your upbringing determines how you grow. Obviously, you have Devon's skills at computing, but you don't share his values. You have been weakened by being raised by normal humans."

"I don't think it's a weakness to have values," Tristan snapped.

"The *wrong* values," Montoya corrected him. "You've been raised poorly. You act emotionally, instead of rationally. You should be like your clone brother — on our side. You should be working for Quietus, not against it."

"Quietus wants to destroy the human race," Tristan said bitterly. "I will never help them in that aim."

"We aim to *save* the human race," the judge insisted. She was clearly trying to justify her beliefs now, not simply answer questions. Like most fanatics, she had a need to be understood. "We are only working at wiping out the diseased portion of the race. The part that depends on the Net for everything, instead of being strong in themselves."

"That's just about everyone on Earth," Mora pointed out, appalled.

"True." Montoya shrugged. "But it is necessary, in order to correct what has gone wrong. For far too long, the strong have supported and coddled the weak. And what happened? The weak have sapped the strength of the strong, weakening them, too. Now that must stop. The Doomsday Virus will wipe out WorldNet, and bring the corrupt, diseased order crashing down. Quietus and the strong will survive. Once the weak have died out, we will rebuild Earth." She smiled smugly. "We shall take Mars as our base, and wait while Earth goes through its death throes. Then we shall return, reclaim the world, and rebuild."

Tristan was at a loss for words; she was talking about killing off the majority of the human race! Genia wasn't so silent.

"You horrible woman!" she snapped. "Anyone you disapprove of will die? You're the sick one!"

"And you are one of the doomed," the judge said complacently. "All of you are the sort of creatures dragging the human race down. The ones we don't need. Except maybe Tristan." She stared at him. "You've proven to be more capable than any of us had expected. You've caused us problems, because you should really be one of us. You really should join us."

Tristan was appalled at her attitude. "You still don't get it, do you?" he asked. "If it wasn't for Genia's help, I wouldn't be here. Or Barker. Or Lili. Or even Mora. And my parents — the lowly, noneducated humans that they are — taught me about right and wrong, which is something you clearly don't understand. What you and your colleagues in Quietus want to do is *murder* — on a scale even Hitler or Temba never dreamed about. You're a bunch of sick, sadistic worms hiding behind lofty ideals and fancy phrases. But what it all boils down to is that you want everyone to be like you or else be dead. And that's *wrong*. I'm *glad* that everyone isn't like me. It makes them challenging. It makes life interesting. And they have as much right to their lives as you have to yours."

"Now who's preaching?" Mora snapped. "I thought we were after information."

Tristan flushed, realizing he had gotten a little carried away. "So what is Quietus planning?" he asked the judge. "What is the next step, after taking over Mars?"

"Releasing the Doomsday Virus," she replied.

Tristan scowled. "But I destroyed it, didn't I?"

"Not completely. You did stop it, and wiped it out of the Net. But the Malefactor tricked you into sending it after him. He is not as capable a programmer as you or Devon, but he was able to isolate the Doomsday Virus and has set it breeding."

Tristan stared at her in shock. "He's going to release it again?"

"Yes."

"Doesn't this ever end?" complained Genia. "When will he do this?"

"Once Quietus has secured Mars."

Barker frowned. "They're going to abandon Earth to die and take over Mars," he said. "Is there something happening up there right now?"

"We have started a revolution," Montoya explained. "Soon Mars will be completely under our control."

"And will the rest of Quietus here on Earth skip off and join them?" Lili asked.

"Yes."

Tristan looked at his companions in worry. "But there's nothing we can do to stop them," he protested. "We're not on Mars, and I don't think we know anyone who is."

"Maybe we could warn someone?" Genia suggested.

Barker laughed. "Kid, we're all considered criminals. Who'd listen to *us*?"

Tristan knew he was right; they wouldn't even be given a chance to tell what they knew. Unless . . . An idea started to grow, but he ignored it for the moment. "Well, what we need to know first is who else is in Quietus. We have to stop as many of the top people as possible." He looked at the judge. "How many people are there in Quietus?"

"I don't know."

She was refusing to help again by telling the exact truth. She probably didn't know *exactly* how many members there were. "Hundreds?" he asked. "Or thousands?"

"Thousands," she admitted.

"Oh, great," Mora complained. "The five of us against thousands of them? Tristan, you really *have* flipped."

Genia raised an eyebrow. "Oh, so *now* you believe him? Now you have proof? But you wouldn't believe him before?" Mora flushed, but Tristan couldn't tell if it was from anger or embarrassment. Genia went on. "Does that mean that you don't want to torture him to death any longer for your own sick amusement?"

"No," the judge answered, "I still want to torture him."

"I wasn't talking to you!" Genia exclaimed. "I was talking to Mora."

Tristan was also wondering about Mora, but Barker broke in. "We can work out your personal problems later; while the Truzac's still working, let's milk this filth for everything we can get." He turned to Montoya. "Do you know the names of *any* of the top conspirators in Quietus?"

"Yes," Montoya admitted. "I am known as the Controller. There are also the Malefactor, the Designer, the Rogue —"

"Their *real* names, not their stupid on-line identities!" Barker snapped.

"I know only one real name."

"And what is that?" Tristan demanded.

"Marten Scott."

Genia went pale. "My *father*?" she gasped. Tristan could see her pain, but the judge wasn't at all bothered.

"Is he? I wouldn't know."

Tristan shook his head. "But he's on Ice. In jail!"

"Yes."

Lili moved forward. "Even in jail, he's one of you? How can this be?"

"Because he felt that it was the perfect cover," Montoya answered. "Who would look for him there? He has the run of the place, and a superb computer system. He uses it to do his work. He has neither the need nor the desire to be out among the human race."

"My father . . ." Genia moaned.

Tristan knew what was hurting her about this: her father was a member of Quietus, and Quietus had been behind the attempts to kill her. It was the ultimate act of betrayal from the only parent she had left; he had not simply abandoned her and her mother before Genia was born, but was even now agreeing to have her murdered. Tristan put an arm around her shoulder and felt her shaking. "It'll be all right," he told her.

She shook him off. "It'll be all right," she agreed savagely. "I'm going to *kill* him!"

"No," Barker said. "We need him alive. I can't let you make this personal."

"What are you talking about?" Genia growled. "You don't have any say in this."

"I do now." Barker looked from her to Tristan. "Look, I don't have any great love for the human race. The majority of them have done nothing for me, sending me to the Underworld and then ignoring me. But I've nothing really against it, either. If they weren't so stupid, I'd never have made a living all these years. So I guess I'm in on this mad crusade of yours."

Tristan smiled with relief. "Thanks," he said. "It will make things a lot easier."

Lili grunted. "Much as it's against my own principles, I suppose I'd better help save the dumb world as well." She rolled her eyes. "Only because it's very unlikely I'd ever figure out how to get to Mars in time, anyway." Tristan knew she was covering up what she really felt by pretending to be grouchy, so he thanked her, too.

Then he looked at Mora. He had once thought he knew her better than any other person alive, and that she knew him, too. The past week or so had proven just how wrong he'd been. Looking at her now, he realized he didn't know her at all. Visions of her pretty face had once given him goofy smiles, but looking at it now made him shiver. He'd seen a different Mora, and he no longer knew who or what she was. "How about you?" he asked.

"We don't need her," Genia said promptly. "After all, I don't think we'll have anyone for her to torture, or flies for her to pull wings off of."

Uh-oh . . . It was clear that the two girls didn't like each other at all. But this wasn't the time for fighting among themselves. "She's been made to suffer by Quietus, too," he pointed out. "That gives her the right to choose, I think."

Mora shrugged. "I'm in, I guess. At any rate, I'm not letting any of you out of my sight until I get what I deserve from all of this."

Genia bunched up a fist. "Come here," she said, with mock sweetness. "I can give you that right now."

"Enough!" Barker snapped. "If you want to fight, pick a time and place later. Right now, we've got more important things to do." He turned back to the judge. "Is there anything else that you can tell us that will help us to defeat Quietus?"

"Only that you have less than two days before Quietus is ready to move," she replied. "Then you'll find it's too late to save the precious sheep that you're so concerned about. Look, you're all bright, motivated people. Quietus could use you all. Why not simply join us?"

"Thanks," Tristan said with revulsion, "but I'd sooner have a tazer on my brain."

The judge turned to Barker. "What about you? You don't owe the human race anything; you said so. Why not join the winning side? You could have your pick of the loot when it comes time to reclaim Earth."

"The loot part is tempting," Barker admitted, and Tristan felt a pang of worry. Was the crook going to accept? "The problem is, I don't think I could ever stand the stench of the people I'd have to share it with. No deal." He turned back to Tristan. "So, now what do we do? We can't let this harridan go, since she's going to tell her slimy friends everything if we do."

"I could fix her," Mora said, stepping forward and hefting her tazer. She looked quite eager.

"Somebody calm the psycho babe, all right?" Genia asked scornfully. "Maybe we should drug her or something. She won't be happy until she's hurt someone in a major way."

Tristan almost agreed with her assessment; Mora was showing a very sick desire to hurt people. He supposed he was lucky she was off his case, but he had no intention of letting her loose on even someone like the judge. "I think we should tell the shields," he said. "I can download some of this interview, and that should be enough for them to arrest her."

Genia considered the point. "But some of the shields work for Quietus," she objected. "Those men who tried to kill us on Ice, remember?" How could Tristan forget? "We need somebody we can trust, so I guess it'll have to be Inspector Shimoda."

Tristan hesitated. He knew the suggestion must hurt Genia, since she felt that Shimoda had betrayed her. "Are you sure?"

"Yes." Genia looked disturbed, but adamant. "I still aim to punch her lights out for letting me down, but I'm sure she's honest and reliable. She'll fix the judge, I'll guarantee it."

"Fine." Tristan still had Shimoda's access codes, so he wouldn't have any problems downloading the information.

"Just don't let her have the stuff about my father yet," Genia added. "I think we have to deal with that first."

Tristan gave her a worried look. "Are you sure?"

"Certain." Her face was set. "And it's not just vengeance, either. He probably knows a few more names that we can use. And he's got to have more information than this traitor. We have to get to him first. He might know who the Malefactor is, and we need him to be able to find Devon."

"Right."

Barker nodded to his men. "Tie the judge up, so she'll still be here when the shields come for her," he ordered. Then he grinned at Lili. "Then we go through this house. I'll bet she's got lots of lovely stuff she won't be able to use when she's on Ice . . ." He rubbed his hands together and winked at Tristan. "We may be off to save the world, but I don't see any harm in taking some money for ourselves on the side."

Tristan watched as they headed off to search the house. What a team he'd put together to save the world! A bunch of crooks . . .

But they were all he had.

7

aki Shimoda shifted uncomfortably in her seat as she examined the other people in the room. Some of them would be holographic projections, of course, because most of the members of Computer Control were far too busy to leave their work to attend meetings. It didn't matter how important the meetings were, and this was one of the most vital the group had ever held. They were on the verge of chaos, and something — *anything* — had to be done to stave it off. It was the second time Shimoda had attended such a meeting, but her first since she'd been promoted to head of Security. She'd been nervous the last time she'd been here, and this time she was terrified.

The only person she knew here was Martin Van Dreelen. She still didn't have a clue as to whether she could trust him. Was he the one who'd framed Peter Chen? Or was Chen really guilty?

Around the table were the other ten people who made up Computer Control. Some of them she remembered from her last time here. There was ninety-odd-year-old Dennis Borden, the senior vice president. He looked at least thirty years younger than his age. Shimoda wondered if he knew he'd been cloned. Her first encounter with cloning had been a thug that was a twenty-five-year-old version of him. And she still didn't know whether his DNA had been stolen, or whether he had been trying to give himself a kind of immortality by cloning himself.

Luther Schein sat beside Borden. The sour-faced man was head of Consumer Relations. He didn't look at all happy, which was hardly surprising. He was the one the public interfaced with, and he was taking all the flak for the recent problems. Next to Schein sat Anita Horesh, head of Development. Next to her was Miriam Rodriguez, head of Programming. She was the last one Shimoda recalled speaking at the previous meeting.

The final six were, by and large, silent members of the board. Some through age, some for their own reasons.

Anna Fried was another senior vice president. She had to be about the same age as Borden, and her skin was wrinkled. But her eyes were sharp, and she held a stylus in her fingers that she played with continually. Next was Badni Jada, the man in charge of Personnel. His department was responsible for hiring and staffing, and Shimoda wondered if he knew that some of his choices were working for Quietus. Was he himself one of the enemy?

Ben Quan was head of Finance. He was bland-faced, giving nothing away. Beside him was Therese Copin, who ran Technology. Next was elderly Vladek Cominsky, head of Planning.

At the head of the table was Elinor Morgenstein, the president. For the most powerful person in the world, she looked small and almost mousy. She rarely spoke, but when she did, people listened. Van Dreelen was the voice for the board, and he opened the meeting.

"First of all, I think we should all welcome Taki Shimoda," he said. "Miss Shimoda has become the new head of Security, as you all know, due to the . . . retirement of Peter Chen. It's unfortunate that she's been thrown into the thick of things from her very first day, but I think we all know that we're facing several serious problems at this moment." He turned to Schein. "Luther?"

Schein cleared his throat. "The Administrator of Mars has declared a state of emergency and invoked martial law," he reported uncomfortably. "He requested a special force of shields, which was granted. They are managing to keep order, but trade and normal communications with Syrtis Major and the other cities have been affected."

"How badly?" Miriam Rodriguez demanded.

Schein hesitated for a second. "Very badly. We've been forced to suspend all flights to Mars as of last night. The dock workers went on strike, which precipitated the crisis. No ships are being loaded or unloaded."

"Then why are communications affected?" asked Anita Horesh.

"Unknown," Schein replied. "I suspect the Administrator is keeping a lid on news reports." He glanced at Shimoda. "What do the shields have to say?"

Luckily, Shimoda had been warned by Tamra about the possibility of such questions, and had prepared a response. "The shields were sent by Chen," she answered. "And Chen appears to have been secretly working for Quietus. I cannot vouch for the accuracy of their reports, therefore. However, they do inform me that the situation is being kept in hand, and that the strikes will be stopped."

"But you can't be certain that they're telling the truth?" Borden snapped.

Shimoda shook her head. "I can't be certain that *anyone* is telling the truth," she said slowly. "Including the members of this board." She swallowed as she said this, nervous and worried. She didn't expect that to go down well.

Nor did it. There were sharp intakes of breath and several muttered curses. Then Cominsky glared at her. "Are you saying that there may be other traitors among us?"

"No — I'm saying there *are* other traitors among us." Shimoda was going out on a limb here, but she knew she was right. It was the only thing that made sense; Quietus had to have help from Computer Control, and not simply Chen. She avoided looking at Van Dreelen. "We cannot trust everything that is spoken here."

"This is outrageous!" Schein snapped. "If you have proof that one or more of us is a traitor, then present it! Otherwise —"

"If she had proof," Van Dreelen said sharply, "then the guilty person would have been arrested, you idiot. I've been working very closely with Miss Shimoda —"

"So I noticed," Horesh muttered.

"And I've seen the same data she has," Van Dreelen continued, ignoring the snide comment. "I'm inclined to agree with her: There is at least one more member of this body who is secretly working for Quietus."

"You just like being a thorn in everyone's side," Jada stated. "What proof do you have?"

Shimoda leaned forward. "Judge Montoya has just been arrested," she reported. "She has confessed under Truzac to being a member of Quietus, and she claimed that her contact is someone on this board."

"Chen, obviously," Rodriguez said. "She worked with him, after all."

"And she sentenced Chen to life on Ice," Van Dreelen pointed out. "Would she have done that if he were her only contact here?"

"Can we believe her accusations?" asked Jada.

"They were given under Truzac," Van Dreelen said.

"And why was she given Truzac in the first place?" asked Morgenstein abruptly. It was the first time the president had spoken. "I don't recall being notified until less than an hour ago that she had been arrested."

Shimoda licked her lips, and tried to contain her nervousness. "We didn't administer the drug," she answered, trying to keep her voice authoritative. "I was sent a computer file showing her interrogation."

"By whom?" the president demanded.

"A group of wanted criminals," Shimoda admitted.

"Criminals?" Horesh yelled. "And you *believe* them?"

"Yes," Shimoda said stubbornly. It was too late to back down now. "One of them is the girl Genia, who helped me to track down the source of the Doomsday Virus. Technically, she's a criminal, but I believe she is reliable."

"Do you?" asked Morgenstein frostily. "You may now be head of Security, Miss Shimoda" — she glared at Van Dreelen; obviously she hadn't exactly approved of the promotion — "but you are not expected to determine guilt or innocence alone. That is the job of the courts."

"The court headed by Montoya," Shimoda pointed out, "who has confessed to being an agent of Quietus. I move that we cannot trust any of her decisions, and all her cases should be reexamined."

"That would be . . . virtually impossible," Borden exclaimed. "There must be hundreds of them!"

"Would you rather see innocent people languish in jail or in the Underworld?" asked Van Dreelen. "Just because it's *inconvenient* to give them justice?"

Borden flushed. "Of course not," he agreed. "But . . . we must be *sure* of all of this before we suggest any such sweeping changes."

"We are certain," Shimoda said. "And I have already

assigned agents to check the cases, starting with the most recent. They are the most likely to be corrupted by her allegiance to Quietus. I have personally appealed her judgment in the case of Genia." That was one of the privileges of rank; now all she needed to do was find the girl and inform her that she would be free again!

"If this is true," Morgenstein said, "then your actions are commendable. However, it seems to me that there are serious problems here. You already stated that there must be at least one more traitor in our midst; how can we be certain that it isn't you?"

Shimoda had been expecting this. From her brief-case, she took a single dose of Truzac and laid it before her on the table. "I am willing to inject myself with this and then answer any questions you may have," she said. "That will prove my loyalty is to Computer Control and not to Quietus."

"*If* that really contains Truzac," Copin said.

Shimoda smiled. "I'll inject you instead," she suggested. "And then we'll ask you the same questions." She looked around the board. "How many of you are willing to come down here and take Truzac and be questioned as to your loyalties?"

Van Dreelen shook his head. "Taki," he said gently, "I already told you that we cannot force anyone to take Truzac. It's against the Constitution."

"I'm not forcing anyone," Shimoda answered. "I'm calling for volunteers. I'm inclined to believe that anyone who voluntarily subjects themselves to the truth drug is innocent. And anyone who refuses is bound to raise suspicions."

"This is demeaning," Quan snapped. "We are being treated like common criminals. Van Dreelen is right — we do not have to agree to this. I, for one, will not be treated like a common thief."

"Nobody's accusing you of being a *common* thief," Van Dreelen said maliciously. "An uncommon one, perhaps." He glanced at Shimoda. "I think our newest member is perhaps a trifle too enthusiastic."

"Perhaps so," Shimoda said stubbornly. "But isn't it better to *know* who we can trust than to sit here and argue about whether it's beneath our dignity to take Truzac?"

"You go too far," Jada insisted. "This is your first meeting, and you accuse us of being traitors, or worse, on the word of a corrupt judge and a thief? I move that she be replaced, effective immediately."

Shimoda had been afraid that someone would do this, but she knew she didn't dare back down now. "And why would you demand that?" she asked sweetly. "Because you don't want your secrets known?" Jada flushed and started to protest.

"Enough," Morgenstein decided coldly. She glared at Shimoda, and Shimoda winced. She had a strong suspicion what would come next. The president could overrule Van Dreelen's appointment anytime she wished. . . . "Miss Shimoda is certainly overstepping her authority," the president said firmly. "But she is doing it out of passion, clearly, and not out of malice. I will not agree to any challenge of her in this matter."

Shimoda could hardly believe her ears; the president was backing her up? "However," Morgenstein continued, "I agree with Martin that we cannot be subject to questioning under Truzac. That would make our meetings an utter farce." She gestured at the sprayer. "Put that away."

Shimoda obeyed, her heart sinking again. Morgenstein had defused the one way of possibly finding the truth, but at least she'd backed Shimoda's appointment. It was impossible to tell her motivation, though.

Morgenstein looked around the meeting. "Earth is in crisis," she stated. "I wish there was another word for it, but there is not. The Martian situation is not good, but that is a matter the Administrator must handle himself. If he requests aid, we will, of course, consider it. Meanwhile, Miss Shimoda will proceed with reevaluating Judge Montoya's cases. If any further *reliable* evidence against any member of this board is raised, then

I will authorize questioning under Truzac. Otherwise, we will assume that we are all innocent of any involvement with subversive groups. Due to the state of matters, our next meeting will be held in twenty-four hours. For now, you are all dismissed."

Shimoda sat back in her seat, feeling more than a little stunned by everything. The board members started to leave, all silently, either in person or else simply by turning off their projected images. In a few moments, she was left alone with Van Dreelen and Morgenstein.

"Martin," the president said, "I have to confess that I was against your decision to appoint this woman to Peter's place. She seems to be very young and tactless."

Van Dreelen grinned. "I thought those were her strong points," he said.

Morgenstein actually cracked a smile. "Perhaps you're correct." She turned to Shimoda. "You handled yourself very well, even if that Truzac stunt was a trifle foolish. You didn't really expect anyone to agree to take it, did you? The members of this board tend to be very proud, and stand on their dignity."

"When they don't sit on it," Van Dreelen muttered.

"I had hoped some would agree," Shimoda said honestly. "I was in earnest about taking it myself."

"Because you're young, innocent, and without too

much self-pride," Morgenstein pointed out. "Unlike the rest of us. The members of this board are the most powerful people in the world, child, and the thought of being treated like common criminals is too galling for them to take."

"One or more of them — of *us* — *is* a common criminal," Shimoda pointed out.

"And the moment you discover who that is, you can arrest them and do with them whatever you wish," the president assured her. "But not before." Abruptly, she smiled again. "I suspect I'm going to like having you on the board, Taki. Things have never been so lively before."

Shimoda realized this was a dismissal, so she nodded and hurried out. She hadn't discovered anything really new at the meeting, but at least she now had a good idea of who her suspects were. She only wished she knew how many of the eleven other members she could trust. . . .

8

evon was getting slightly bored with being the boss. Now that he'd won, he discovered that *having* wasn't what he wanted, after all. What he enjoyed was the *winning*. The game was no fun once it was over. Besides, there wasn't a whole lot he could do with the Moon. Armstrong City was okay as far as it went, but ruling a bunch of moles living in tunnels inside the Moon wasn't really all that thrilling.

He had to do something to make life more interesting again. He actually considered handing power back to the governor, just so he could steal it again, but that would simply be repeating what he already knew was possible. There really wasn't much fun in that.

"It's not fair," he muttered. "Winning should be more fun than this." He stared at his Screens, watching the people go about their dull, meaningless lives. Maybe a disaster would amuse him? He could turn off the air in the living tunnels, maybe? Killing a few hundred people might be fun. But he really didn't think so. There wasn't any challenge in any of this. He wished he could peer into their homes, and watch their boring lives unfold. He'd really enjoyed doing that on Earth. Seeing how deadly dull most people's lives were made him better appreciate his own fortune and genius. But the apartments on the Moon didn't have security monitors, as they did on Earth, so that wasn't possible. The only room he could watch was the governor's office, and there was really very little fun in watching that fat, stupid man sweat. Devon knew, because he'd been doing it long enough.

On the other hand, since *he* was in charge of the Moon now, he could order changes made, couldn't he?

"Governor!" Devon called out, and grinned as the terrified man snapped to attention on the Screen.

"Yes?" he squeaked. "What is it?"

"I've decided that there's going to be a new law,"

Devon informed him. "Starting today, everyone has to install at least one security monitor in their homes. I want them linked into the security monitoring system, so I can watch people when I feel like it."

"Ah . . ." The governor was rubbing his hands together. "That might not be a good idea."

"What?" Devon glowered at the man. "If I want it, then it *must* be a good idea. Surely you agree?"

"Well, yes, normally I would," the man spluttered. "Only . . ."

"Only *what*?"

"Well, it's just that people on the Moon are very independent," the governor explained. "When the colony was founded, they decided they didn't want monitors."

"Well, that's their tough luck, isn't it?" Devon snapped. "I don't care *what* they decided before I took power; now that I'm in charge, they'll do just what I tell them. Haven't you understood that yet?"

"There will be some complaints," the Governor protested.

"If they don't do it, there will be some *deaths*," Devon promised. "In fact, that's how you can convince them to do it. Tell them it's for their own safety."

"They won't believe me," the governor objected.

"Then I'll just have to kill a few people until they *do* believe you, won't I?" Devon suggested.

"No, no, that won't be necessary!"

"Then *do* it!" Devon insisted. "If I can't start access-ing people's homes by this time tomorrow, I'll start picking victims."

"It'll take some time!" the governor protested.

"It had better not," Devon warned him. "I don't expect to see everyone all at once. But you'd better have the first ones up by tomorrow, and then the rest of the colony by the end of the month. Or the deaths will be on your head. I hear elections are coming up, and you wouldn't want to get voted out of office, would you?"

"As if that would matter," the governor muttered.

"It would matter to me," Devon told him. "I like you working for me. It might take some time to break in an-other flunky. But I'll do it if I have to. You could always have a fatal accident, you know."

There was a buzz at the governor's door. "I have to get that," the man said.

"Go ahead," Devon said. "Just remember, I'll be watching you. So be good."

The governor was sweating again, which made Devon grin. He tapped the button to open his door, and Moss entered. Moss was the governor's secretary and right-hand man. Unlike the governor, he was a worker, and he had some brains. He kept track of what the governor needed. Devon had already been raiding the man's files, and found them most helpful.

"Governor," Moss said, and then blinked. "Are you all right, sir? You look rather . . . ill."

"I'm fine," the governor lied. He could hardly reveal the truth. "What did you want to see me about?"

"Computer Control on Earth contacted us a short while ago, sir. Apparently there is trouble on Mars. Strikes and unrest. The Administrator there has declared a state of emergency."

"Well, that's a shame, but it's hardly news," the governor replied. "We heard about this yesterday."

"There's been a new development," Moss explained. "All shipping has been stopped. Anything in transit is being rerouted here. We're likely to have about two dozen extra ships coming in. Some will be loading or unloading, others just getting ready to return to Earth."

"Well, then, see to it," the governor said, waving his hand dismissively. "I'm sorry for their troubles, but we have our own."

"Really?" Moss raised his eyebrows. "And what might they be?"

The governor had obviously just been talking without thinking, but he caught himself well. "New regulations from Earth," he lied. "In the last batch of messages. I just found it. Apparently some sort of insurance regulations, but we now have to install security monitors in every apartment." He sighed rather convincingly. "More red tape and trouble. Do we have the supplies and manpower to manage this?"

"I'll have to check, sir," Moss said, looking worried. "But . . . that sounds like an unpopular idea to me, sir. You know how Lunies don't like the idea of being rigidly controlled. This could cost you the next election."

"Do you think I don't know this?" the governor asked. "But I have to obey legislation. You know that. If there are complaints, apologize for me, but point that out."

"Very good, sir." Moss looked at the door. "Will that be all for now?"

"I think so, yes."

Moss left the room, and something about his manner made Devon chuckle. The man looked very conspiratorial. Tapping into the secretary's computer, Devon waited. Sure enough, a moment later, Moss came online and started hunting through the governor's correspondence. Devon grinned. The secretary didn't believe his boss, and was checking for that nonexistent order from Earth! For a moment, Devon was tempted to fake one and put it into the governor's files. Then he stopped, his hand just above his speedboard.

No! That wouldn't be as much fun! Let Moss think the governor was lying. It would be much more interesting if he *couldn't* find that order! Maybe Moss would start a campaign against the governor, or even try to delay the work. The governor knew he had a deadline, and that Devon wasn't bluffing about killing people to enforce it. If Moss caused problems, it would give the governor a fit. That would be fun to watch.

In fact, maybe Devon could cause a slowdown himself, just to see how the governor would panic. That was worth a thought! Sabotage the governor, and then punish him for failing . . .

This was starting to get very amusing again.

But Moss actually did start the work orders going for the monitoring cameras, and ordered a work crew to begin installation. Since the work area was a public place, there was already a camera there. Devon brought that picture up on his screen.

Two of the workmen started to get a small electric cart ready, loading cameras and components onto it, along with their toolboxes. "This isn't going to be popular," one of the men said with certainty.

"So what?" his friend answered. "It's nothing to do with us. We were just told to do the work. They can't blame us for it. They voted this moron into office, not me. I always thought he was dumber than my son's collection of Moon rocks."

"Well, he certainly seems to be proving it," the other

man answered. Their cart loaded, they climbed aboard and drove it to their assigned work area. Devon followed their progress on the public cameras, grinning happily. There was going to be trouble, he was sure of that.

And he was right. The first apartment they stopped at was owned by a small family. The father was at work, but the mother was home with a baby. She answered the door and scowled at the two workers. "I didn't send for maintenance."

"You didn't have to," the heavier man answered. "New regulations. We've got to install a security camera inside your apartment."

"What?" The woman's eyes narrowed. "Over my dead body!"

If you like, Devon thought, his fingers hovering over his controls. It would be a simple matter to lock her in her apartment and turn off the heat. She and her baby would freeze in a very short time. The only thing spoiling the fun would be that Devon wouldn't be able to watch them die.

"We've got our orders, ma'am," the thinner man said. "If you give us grief, we'll get into trouble with the governor. If you don't like the regulation, you can protest directly to him, you know."

"And I shall!" the woman snapped. She stared at the

men. "Well, I suppose you can start, at least, while I complain. But you'd better be ready to take it with you when you leave!" She stormed over to her Terminal and tried to dial the governor. Devon misrouted the call to the sewage processing factory. It was fun hearing her yell and complain at the wrong man, as if it was his fault. Then she tried again, and he sent the message to the local NewsNet. The reporter was interested in her complaint, though, and promised to get to the bottom of it.

Devon let her third call go through to the governor. Then he watched as more calls backed up. Everyone, it seemed, wanted to complain about the new rule, and the NewsNet wanted to post an exposé of the governor's lust for power.

This was definitely getting to be more fun again!

Devon sat back, chuckling to himself. He'd really managed to hit on a good idea this time. But what could he do once the amusement from this wore off?

He'd think of something. . . .

9

Genia sat in the back of the hovercraft, brooding. She had thought that she'd been through so much that nothing could get through her defenses again. How wrong could she get? Her own father had been one of the people trying to kill her — and to take over the world!

Okay, she'd never been close to her father. In fact, she'd only seen him while she was on Ice. But she had thought he felt *something* for her, even if it was only guilt. And it looked now like he'd been simply playing her for a fool. Genia had believed that her inner core was too tough to be hurt again, but she was wrong. Her stomach was churning, and she ached all the way to her bones. Miserably, she sat there feeling sorry for herself.

It didn't help that the others kept trying to comfort her. They wouldn't believe that she didn't want their kind words, and that she just wanted to be left alone. Even Barker had tried to sound sympathetic, and a day or so back he had been trying to rob her blind. Tristan had tried the hardest, of course, since that was how Tristan was — soft, through and through. Genia appreciated that he meant well, but he really didn't have a clue how she felt.

Now, it appeared, it was Mora's turn to try. Mora, of all people! The other girl approached Genia's isolated seat with hesitation, but she managed to force her feet to bring her over. She sat beside Genia and stared forward, not even trying to look her in the eyes.

"Do you hate me?" she asked abruptly.

It wasn't what Genia had been expecting. "Huh? Why should I hate you? You've only been a miserable, sadistic little witch who threatened to torture or kill me. Heck, that's one of the nicest things anyone's ever said to me."

"I guess I deserve that sarcasm," Mora admitted. "I *have* behaved very badly."

"Badly?" Genia stared at the girl. "Badly is when you

tell me I'm dressed like a tramp, or that this shade of face paint is wrong for my hair. *Badly* doesn't even begin to cover what you've done."

Mora sighed. "You're right. But it's so much easier for you than it is for me."

Genia shook her head in astonishment. "What are you talking about?"

"Well, you've never had anything in your life, except for what you've worked for. Me, I lived a privileged life, where I was given anything I needed. Pampered, I suppose you'd call it. And when I lost everything that I knew, I guess I lost control of myself, too. I couldn't deal with having *nothing*. You can."

Genia glared at her.

"I meant it as a compliment."

"You have a funny choice in compliments," Genia snapped.

"I meant that you're stronger than me," Mora answered. "I admire you for that. I'm not strong at all. I buckled when I lost my old life. I wanted revenge on Tristan to make somebody pay for what I'd lost. I blamed him for everything."

"And now you feel like a jerk, because it wasn't his fault?" Genia suggested. "That boy has done everything he could to help everyone in this mess. He just won't give up. He's determined to save the human race, even if they all think he's a crook and want him locked away for life. And instead of helping him and believing him, you turned him in and then blamed him for your own failures. You're a miserable failure as a human being, you know that?"

"It's becoming painfully obvious," Mora confessed.

"Oh good." Genia shrugged. "You know something? My problems don't seem to be quite as bad now that I've told you what an utter failure you are. My father wants to kill me, the shields want to send me to jail for life, and I'm stuck talking to a moron like you. Hey, I can deal with that. At least I'm *not* a moron like you."

Mora winced. "I suppose I deserve that. But I just want to make amends. I'm sorry for how I treated you before, and I want to make up for it."

Genia grinned nastily. "Well, you could start by sticking that tazer of yours to your head and pulling the trigger. I'd feel a lot happier about you if you were no longer around."

Mora bit her lip. "Can't we be friends?" she asked plaintively.

Genia laughed. "Wow, you really *have* cheered me up. Maybe Barker can appoint you his court jester or something — you're so funny. *Friends?* Buy a clue, stupid!" She leaned forward. "You know that old proverb about forgiving and forgetting?" Mora nodded. "I hate it. I *never* forgive, and I'll *never* forget."

Mora glared back at her. "Is that what I get for trying to make up?" she asked.

"Think yourself lucky," Genia suggested. "I could have gone with my first impulse and simply punched you in the mouth. Now, if you don't mind, I'd like to get back to brooding about my father."

Mora stood up. "I don't know what Tristan sees in you!"

Genia snorted. "Probably as little as I see in him, sweetheart. We're just working together, not planning on getting bonded. Get over this jealousy thing of yours, okay? If you want him back, be my guest. And if he takes you back, he's a bigger fool than I think he is. And, trust me, that's a pretty big fool already."

"You hate *everyone*, don't you?" Mora snapped.

"Of course not," Genia answered. "I don't *know* everyone. I just hate the ones I do know."

Mora shook her head and flounced off in a huff. Going to try to smooth things over with Tristan, probably. Genia wondered if it would work. Would Tristan take Mora back, after everything she'd done? Knowing what an idealistic idiot Tristan was, that wasn't out of the scope of possibility. Still, what difference did that make to *her*? She wasn't interested in Tristan as anything other than a partner until they both cleared their names. After that, she'd be glad to see the back of the kid. Even if he was kind of attractive. And considerate. And sort of nice . . .

What was wrong with her? "Are you *asking* to be hurt?" she questioned herself quietly. First of all, she'd trusted a shield, of all people! And then felt hurt when Inspector Shimoda had let her down! What a jerk she was sometimes. To feel like a shield would care about her, and actually try to keep her word. Well, to be honest, Genia could see that her being sent to Ice wasn't really Shimoda's fault. There hadn't been anything the shield could do about it. But it still felt like she'd been let down somehow. And that was dumb. Shimoda didn't owe Genia anything. So what if she'd failed?

Yet Genia still felt as if she could trust Shimoda. Why else had she sent the woman that data on the judge and Quietus's plans? Genia was sure that Shimoda would believe her and trust her, even after what had happened.

Maybe she was cracking up.

And now she was starting to *like* Tristan Connor. That was crazy. She'd only survived this long by staying strong, staying alone. She could never trust anyone else to care about her. They all let her down, sooner or later. Starting with her father. Why was she so surprised that he wanted her dead? He'd abandoned her before she was born, expecting her to die now. Why was she feeling so hurt and betrayed? She should know better.

None of her thinking helped. She was bitterly angry at her father. As for Mora . . . Well, she didn't hate the other girl, actually. She pitied her, mostly. It couldn't be easy living life with such a shallow mind. And, to be honest, she was kind of envious of her. Mora's life had been everything that Genia's hadn't — she'd had a family, love, comfort, security . . . and Tristan. Genia didn't *need* any of that, of course . . . but it might have been nice to have it anyway.

A while later, Tristan came back from the cabin. Genia roused herself from her brooding, wondering what he and Mora had been up to all this time. She realized that she felt a pang of jealousy, which was absurd. She *really* was going to have to watch her emotions; they were getting quite out of hand!

"We're almost there," he informed her, sitting beside her. "Barker's taking us the last part of the way. I thought we'd better get ready." He sighed. "I hate the idea of going back to Ice again, but we really don't have a choice, do we?"

"You've always had a choice," she answered, seriously for once. "Tristan, why do you do it?"

"Do what?"

"You're risking your life to save a lot of people who don't care about you. You don't owe them anything. Just because the person behind all of this is your clone twin doesn't mean you have to take him out. That's the shields' job, not yours."

"They can't do it," Tristan said simply. "I'm the only one with the skills to do it. With your help, of course."

"You don't have to patronize me!" Genia snapped. "You don't need me, and we both know it. You could fix Devon all by yourself."

"Maybe I could," Tristan agreed. He looked confused and surprised by her comment. As if he didn't actually believe she was right. "But I doubt it. You're a big help to me — not least due to your hostility." He grinned. "It keeps me on edge, and stops me getting too full of myself. Plus, you're the most capable person I've known in my entire life. No matter what happens, you never give up."

For some reason Genia wanted to scream or cry, and she didn't know why. "I come very close to giving up," she confessed. Why was she baring her soul like this to him?

"But you don't give in," he said firmly. "I don't know anyone else who'd agree to go back to the worst jail on Earth to try to save people who want her back inside."

"Don't make me sound so noble," Genia groused.

"I'm returning to get back at my father, that's all. I should have made him pay when we were here before; he's not getting off this time."

"If that's what you want to believe," Tristan said amiably. "I know you better than that, though. You're not as tough and uncaring as you make out."

"Yes, I am," she insisted, but she couldn't help being touched by his faith in her. "You're in for a shock if you think otherwise."

"Maybe. Anyway, don't forget, we want to break your father out of Ice to question him, not to kill him."

Genia snorted. "Are you confusing me with your *girlfriend*?" she mocked him. "I have no intention of killing my father. I want him to *suffer*, not to die."

"Information first, suffering later," Tristan said.

"Speaking of which and whom," Genia said, changing the subject slightly. "Are you and Mora an item again?" There was a tightness in her chest, though she managed to make the enquiry sound casual. What was *wrong* with her?

"No."

Genia felt relieved, but she still scowled. "Didn't she try?"

"Yes."

She raised an eyebrow and looked at him. "It's not like you to be so monosyllabic."

Tristan sighed. "Look, I still find Mora attractive — I guess I'd have to be dead not to. But . . . I'm very disturbed with her recent behavior. I just can't bring myself to trust her again." He patted her hand. "It's very sweet of you to want to get us together again, but it's not going to work, I'm afraid."

Genia was astonished. Is *that* what he thought she was doing? Actually, she was *glad* Tristan hadn't taken Mora back. How could Tristan be so blind? Because he was Tristan, of course. He always thought the best of other people, and assumed they were all acting as unselfishly as he did. "So now what?" she asked. Was she hoping he'd find *her* attractive instead? *Get real, Genia!* she ordered herself.

"Now we save the world, I guess. Business as usual." He grinned, getting to his feet. "We'd better get ready."

Genia felt inexplicably disappointed by his reaction. Didn't he like her at least a little? Was he just being shy? Or was she being stupid? *Face it,* she told herself. *You're a thief, a cheat, and a nobody from the Underworld. Why would anyone be interested in you romantically?* She got to her feet and went with him to the storage bay, struggling with her unfocused emotions.

Barker had come through again. Once he'd agreed to commit himself to helping, the crook had worked hard.

He'd stocked them up with supplies and weapons. Tristan struggled into a cold-weather suit and goggles to protect against the bitter chill of Antarctica. Genia did likewise, and then both started loading up with weapons.

They wouldn't be able to use the same trick to get back in as they had to escape. The shields weren't stupid, so they were bound to have made sure the knockout gas wouldn't work a second time against them. Barker had suggested a small bomb to get in, but Tristan had been against this, since it would wound or kill innocent shields. That hadn't worried Barker too much, but Genia had agreed with Tristan: No innocent people were to get hurt. Barker had sighed, and given in.

Lili's medical knowledge had come through again. Instead of tazers, they all carried tranquilizer guns. She'd whipped up a knockout drug that took effect the moment it hit any unprotected skin. Genia was amused that their weapons were effectively water pistols — firing a stream of the trank in short bursts. Each gun carried enough for a hundred such shots.

Getting into Ice, of course, wasn't going to be so simple. This part was Genia's responsibility, and she was going to have fun with it. She packed the equipment she needed in her backpack.

Barker joined them. "Lili's at the controls," he said.

One of his men was with him, and the two men started getting dressed quickly and efficiently. "She and Mora are staying with the craft, ready for a fast getaway once we have Scott."

"I feel a lot safer knowing Mora isn't with us," Genia muttered. Everyone ignored her, though they must have heard her comment.

"We're only a hundred yards from the entrance," Barker said. "I just hope that jammer you came up with works, Genia."

"If it didn't, we'd have been attacked by now." Genia grinned, but they couldn't see her face, of course.

"Okay." Barker hefted his trank rifle. "Let's do it, then."

His thug triggered the door, which opened into a howling whiteness. The man plunged out, and Genia followed. Tristan came next, while Barker brought up the rear. It was like walking into a thick cloud — she couldn't see more than a few feet in the wind-whipped snow. She had to follow the man ahead of her as fast as possible. She prayed that he knew where he was going.

The wind tried to knock her down and pummel her into the rock under her feet. There was a slick of ice over the rock, and without her boots she'd have been sliding away. Leaning forward, she moved on, following the barely visible form of the thug. After a few moments, the larger bulk of the entrance to Ice came into view. Genia pressed against the wall, sheltered for the time being from the terrible wind. Reaching into her pack, she pulled out her hand-comp, which was inside a vacuum seal bag to protect it from the snow and ice.

Extending the hand-comp's two probes, she managed to attach them on the second attempt to the entrance lock. Then she started her decoding program, which worked out the correct entry codes. It took almost two minutes — two very uncomfortable minutes. Despite the protective gear she wore, she could still feel the chill starting to creep in and attack her.

Then the hand-comp chimed — barely audible in this gale — and the door was unlocked. Barker and his man took over, nodding signals to each other. Then they threw open the door and charged inside. Genia and Tristan followed, with Tristan shutting the door behind them.

The two guards were already unconscious as Genia and Tristan entered, and Barker's man had the elevator door to the depths open. They piled inside, and set it going down. Barker and his helper were in front, their trank rifles at the ready. When the door hissed open, they fired at the two startled shields waiting for the elevator. The two men collapsed onto the floor, and Barker paused only long enough to grab the electronic key from the first man.

"Come on," he said, urgently. "Our luck can't hold for too long. They have to be monitoring events."

That was Tristan's cue. He plugged his own hand-comp into the guard station, and promptly shut down all the security monitors. Working feverishly, he then sealed all the doors, except the ones that they would need. "Done," he said. "They're isolated."

"Gas filters," Barker ordered, slipping the flat disc over his own nose and mouth. The shields were bound to release the riot gas as soon as they knew there was a problem. The filters would enable the intruders to withstand it, thanks to Lili's planning.

The four of them went through the doorway into the main portion of the prison. There were several prisoners already collapsed, sleeping from the effects of the gas. "The shields are very efficient," Barker noted. "Let's move it before they break Tristan's codes."

Genia led the way back to the cell where her father lived. They passed through the stone-hewed corridors, and more sleeping prisoners. The shields were taking no chances now, it seemed. Reaching the cell, she saw the door was closed. Barker's man moved in and pushed it open, against some resistance. Genia saw that it was his father's second wife, Sarai, who'd fallen down unconscious behind the door. On an impulse, she pointed at the woman. "Bring her, too."

"We don't need extra weight," Barker objected.

"She'll serve to put pressure on my father," Genia said.

"Fair enough." Barker bent and slung the woman over his shoulder. His man emerged from the cell a moment later, a male form draped over his shoulder.

"Hang on," Genia said, wanting to be certain. She grabbed the man by the hair and jerked his head up so she could look at it. Marten Scott's unconscious face stared back at her. "Yes, that's the right villain," she agreed. "Let's go."

With Barker and his man both burdened, it was up to Genia and Tristan to take the lead and watch for trouble. Their way back to the elevator was clear, though, and the doors still open.

Something struck her as wrong, however, and she signaled a halt. Everything *looked* okay, with the three guards flat out in the corridor. . . .

Three? They'd tranked only two.

"Trouble," she snapped, and opened fire at the supposedly knocked-out guards. One managed to jump to his feet, bringing up his tazer. Genia and Tristan both squirted his face. The man looked astonished, then simply collapsed. The other two didn't even have a chance to get to their feet; the tranks knocked them out as they tried to rise.

Genia led the charge into the elevator, and used her hand-comp to check it out. "Sneaky," she muttered. "There's a concussion grenade looped into the controls. They really *do* learn from their mistakes."

Barker's goon tossed Marten into the elevator, and then jerked the front panel off the controls, exposing the grenade. In a few seconds, he had it defused, and pressed the "up" button. The four of them waited as the elevator rose, wondering what would be waiting for them above. As the doors started to open, tazer blasts slammed into the car.

Genia was already on the floor, however, next to Tristan, and Barker and his man were hiding in the shrinking space behind the opening doors. Genia fired at the shields she could see, as did Tristan. The tazer fire died down, and Barker and his goon leaped out, raking the room with their trank rifles.

"All clear," Barker announced. He snatched up Sarai again, and his man scooped up Marten. Tristan pulled a couple of thermal blankets from his pack, and he and Genia wrapped the two captives. Then, satisfied they wouldn't freeze, he opened the outer door.

There was another shield waiting there, his tazer

aimed. Genia tranked him first, though, and he col-lapsed. Tristan nodded his thanks, and then hauled the unconscious man inside. The four of them left the en-trance, and Tristan sealed the door behind them.

The dash back to the hovercraft was scary; had the shields found it and captured Lili? Would they be ar-rested when they reached it? Would they even find it in this snowy waste? A moment later, Genia made out the shape of it ahead, and Barker and his man plunged in-side. Tristan was next, and Genia stumbled in last, clos-ing the door on the storm.

The ship was silent, the sound of the wind at last cut off. Barker dashed into the cabin, and Genia felt the craft tremble as it started up. Everything was fine, then, and Lili was taking them away from Ice. Genia discov-ered she was shaking from nervous reaction as she tried to peel off her protective gear. The hard part was over — for now, at least.

She joined Tristan and Mora in the main cabin. Sarai and Marten had been dumped in seats, both still out from the riot gas. Mora was using electronic links to bind them in place, which Genia realized was a smart move. They couldn't chance their captives getting free.

She looked down on her father in disgust and tri-umph. He'd abandoned her and then wanted her killed, but he was in her power now. It would be quite a family reunion when he woke up. He was going to regret everything he'd ever done to her; Genia promised herself that.

He was going to pay in blood. . . .

10

himoda stood in her office, though she probably should have been sitting at her desk. It would make her look more respectable, she supposed. But right now she didn't want to look respectable; she wanted to look efficient as she studied the twelve shields in the room with her and Lieutenant Jill Barnes.

"I've been told that I can't make shields take Truzac to find out who's really loyal to us and who is working for Quietus," she explained to the men and women. She shrugged. "Maybe that's true. But there's nothing stopping me from asking for volunteers. Lieutenant Barnes tells me that you've all agreed to take a Truzac test to prove that you're on the side of law and order. If she's wrong, you can leave now." Nobody moved a muscle, and Shimoda felt very relieved. "Good. I'm sorry to have to ask this of you, but we've had so many problems with traitors that I can't assign this mission to anyone I don't have complete confidence in. And I'm not asking you to do anything I'm unwilling to do myself — Lieutenant Barnes and I will also take the test with you, so you can have complete confidence in me." That raised a few eyebrows, as she'd expected.

She moved closer to the agents. "Once you've taken the tests," she said, "you can enroll your own forces. The only condition is that they must agree to the same Truzac test. We're not holding it against anyone who feels they can't take it — but, at the same time, we cannot trust them. They may well be loyal and protesting out of a sense of justice, but I can't help that. They're not getting involved in any of the *real* work here. You can meet with them, of course, but don't *ever* tell them anything that we're doing. That's a direct order, and if anyone disobeys me, they'll be fired. Again, if any of you can't accept that, leave now." Once more, to her relief, nobody stirred. She nodded at her secretary. "Tamra."

Tamra brought out the container of Truzac and the hypo-spray. When she was ready to give the dose, Shimoda took the first one. Then Jill Barnes, and finally the rest of the crew. Tamra asked everyone the same simple question: "Who are you loyal to: the shields or Quietus?" Everyone in the room answered the same way: "The shields."

Shimoda felt considerably better when they were all done. Tamra then surprised her by giving herself a dose. "You'd better ask me the same thing," she said. "After all, you're taking my word for a lot of things." When Shimoda asked, Tamra said firmly: "The shields."

"Good." Shimoda motioned for everyone to relax slightly. "Now, this is very important, and to be kept to ourselves, at least for the time being. There is definitely a traitor on the board of Computer Central. I have suspicions, but no proof at all yet as to who it is. Peter Chen, the old head of Security, was found to be a traitor. Tamra thinks he's innocent and was framed. I've seen the evidence, and it's pretty conclusive."

Tamra frowned. "Does the way you say that, Taki, mean you're *not* convinced he was framed?"

"Oh, I'm convinced the evidence convicting him was faked," Shimoda admitted. "The only thing we don't know is who did it. For all we know, Chen could have framed himself."

"Why would he do that?" asked Tamra, confused.

"I don't know," Shimoda said honestly. "But I

wouldn't put anything at all past Quietus right now. I want you to watch this vid." She triggered her screen, and the copy of the interrogation of Judge Montoya that Genia had sent her played through. When it was finished, Lieutenant Barnes whistled.

"That's bad," she admitted.

"Yes," Shimoda agreed. "And she's the one who sent Chen to Ice." She grinned. "I can't force people to take Truzac," she said, "*unless* they've been accused of a crime. And Chen has been. What I want all of you to do is to go to Ice for me. Take a mess of Truzac, and question Chen. Find out if he really does work for Quietus, or if he's been framed. Then interrogate the shields who tried to kill or free Tristan Connor. Find out what they were doing, who recruited them, and so on. I want everything we can get on Quietus from them. Including whether Tristan Connor works for them or not."

Barnes scowled. "You think he might be innocent?"

"I don't know," Shimoda confessed. She'd been doing a lot of thinking about this. "He was sent to Ice by Montoya, after all. Maybe because she couldn't find a good reason not to send him. Maybe so he could be rescued. Or maybe because Quietus wanted him dealt with. I don't know anymore. I used to think he had to be guilty. But I'm starting to have my doubts." She was still under the influence of the Truzac, so she was telling the absolute truth; but she wasn't telling *all* of it. There was no need to tell everyone that Connor was working with Genia and apparently hunting down Quietus himself. Why would he do that if he was guilty?

Was it possible that he had been telling the truth about that so-called clone of his, Devon? If so, she'd made the biggest blunder of her career, sending an innocent kid to Ice and leaving the *real* saboteur loose.

She had to know the truth. If she could get her hands on Connor again, this time she'd Truzac him without hesitation. If she could find him again, of course. That was easier said than done. She had absolutely no idea where he was right now, and very little chance of finding him without some luck. So she'd do what she could, and that meant probing Chen and the shields on Ice.

She hadn't told Van Dreelen what her plans were, of course. If he complained, she'd think of something to say. But she dared not trust him. He was the most likely person to be a traitor if Chen wasn't. And, more and more, she was believing in Chen's innocence.

Would Chen want his job back if she proved he wasn't guilty? She grinned to herself. He was welcome to it! She wanted to be back on a real case, not trying to figure out who she could trust, and playing politics like this. She wasn't cut out to be behind a desk. She'd much rather be out solving crimes.

"Right," she said. "We start on this immediately. Lieutenant Barnes will lead the raid." She wished she could do it herself, but she'd never be allowed out in the field. "You'll have passes, of course, and the guards on Ice should cooperate fully. But you'd have to be very foolish to assume that they're on our side. So be very, very careful. Cover your backs at all times. And contact me as soon as you have any information. I'll have a direct line to Lieutenant Barnes established and uplinked to my Terminal the whole time. This is our number one priority right now. So, good luck — and get to it."

The shields saluted, and hurried out to get their equipment ready. Shimoda smiled tiredly at her friend. "Be careful, Jill," she warned. "I don't think Quietus knows what we're doing, but they're smarter and sneakier than we possibly know. Take every precaution you can. I'm counting on you."

"I know you are, Taki," Barnes answered, shaking her hand. "And I won't let you down. You'll have some answers in a couple of hours, I promise you that." She left the room.

Tamra tidied away the Truzac. "She's a good shield," she said gently. "She'll do it."

Shimoda sighed. "I want to believe that," she said. "I

really do. This could be our chance to get to the truth at last. But, to be honest, I'm kind of scared about what we'll discover the truth to be." She looked at her secretary with worried eyes. "What do we do when we find out who the traitors are?" She shook her head. "The truth will be only the start of our worries, I promise you that."

11

The Administrator sat in his office feeling very satisfied with himself. He had Mars virtually under his control now, and it was time to move to the next stage. He felt a mild pang of regret that he'd been forced to lock up Charle Wilson; the man was a good worker, but he did seem to have a dreadful streak of morality in him. It was completely misplaced, and the Administrator was pretty sure he could win over his second in command.

Especially once he got hold of the man's wife and children as leverage.

Meanwhile, there was no point in waiting any longer. He turned to his communications Net, and sent the coded signal to Quietus. Because of the time lag for messages to reach Earth, he would have to wait for a reply. But his message out was going to be positive and upbeat. He felt a tremendous sense of achievement.

"Administrator to the Rogue," he recorded. "Mars is now secure, and we are awaiting the arrival of the Synod. I can assure you of a fine reception, while we wait for the destruction of the old and the birth of our new world order." There! That should do it. Not too pompous, but cheery and welcoming. He transmitted the signal, and then sat back to wait for Quietus's reply.

It made him proud to know that he was such an integral part of the victory. Without him, Quietus would never have been able to stage their grand design. When the members of the Synod arrived, he'd be the hero of the day. He had everything ready for them, and the few minor glitches would be solved by the time the members of Quietus reached Mars.

He was still considering the glory that would be his when the Rogue replied. She was masked by the holo-projector, as always; until the coup was successful, it was important that as few people as possible knew the identities of the Synod members. The Administrator himself knew only the person who'd recruited him and none of the others, which was as it should be. He'd always fantasized that the Rogue was beautiful, though, and that she would be swept off her feet by him when she reached his Mars.

"Administrator," she said warmly, "Quietus is very pleased with your progress. You've managed to bring the schedule back on track, despite our recent setbacks. I am convening a meeting of the Synod immediately, and we shall set a time now for our evacuation to join you on Mars. My congratulations once again, and I look forward to seeing you in person very shortly. Rogue out."

The Administrator sat back in his chair, extremely happy. The Rogue was looking forward to seeing him! Perhaps his dreams would come true after all. Not only the launch of the revitalized human race, but perhaps a wedding in his own future . . .

The desk communicator chimed, breaking into his thoughts. Dragging himself back to reality, the Administrator tapped the switch. "What is it?"

"Barstow," came the reply. He was the head of the force sent to arrest Wilson's family. "The domicile is empty. The family isn't here."

The Administrator felt a pang of anger, but this was just a minor delay. "Then *find them*, you idiot," he snapped. "They can't have left the city, with the curfew on. I want them tracked down and brought in. *Do it!*" He snapped off the link. The morons! Did he have to do *all* of the thinking around here? The Administrator went back to work, placing the problem in the back of his mind. It was almost insignificant, after all. . . .

Two hours later, his assistant buzzed him. Halting the program he was working through, the Administrator took the call. "What is it?" he demanded. "How can I get any work done with all of these interruptions?"

"You'd better check your Screen, sir," the man answered. He sounded nervous and worried. "The public news channel."

The Administrator scowled. "I believe I ordered that shut down for the duration," he said menacingly. If someone had failed him . . .

"You did, sir, and it was," his assistant answered quickly. "But you'd better watch the channel all the same."

With a growl, the Administrator turned on his wall Screen. He flicked it to the public news channel. As his assistant had said, it was anything but closed down.

The face of Captain Montrose filled the Screen, caught in midspeech. The man was the head of the local shields, and the Administrator had judged him unreliable, bypassing his authority and ordering him to work with the imported Earth shields. What did the man think he was doing?

". . . Illegal actions," Montrose was saying. "He has set the Earth shields to attack Martian citizens, and has arrested deputy administrator Wilson without cause. Under his authority, several Martian workers have been massacred, and he is working with a foreign power to deliver Mars into their hands."

Montrose was talking about him, the Administrator realized with a shock. Telling *everyone* what was happening! He stabbed at his communicator buttons feverishly.

"The Administrator is betraying the people of Mars, and we, your shields, cannot stand back and let this happen. We are pledged to fight to restore democracy to Mars, and we ask every able-bodied person to join with us in resisting these illegal and immoral actions."

"What's going on?" the Administrator shouted at his assistant. "How can this be going out? I want it shut down immediately!"

"We . . . can't stop it, sir," the man apologized. "Somehow, the rebels have hacked into the computer systems. There are so many bugs and pitfalls that our technicians are having terrible trouble getting anywhere. We can shut it down eventually, but it may take an hour or so."

"An hour or so?" The Administrator gestured at the Screen, where Montrose was going on further about the rebellion, issuing a general call to arms. "That man is talking treason, and I want him stopped, now!" He stabbed at the buttons again, getting the captain of the shields who had been sent to him from Earth. "Montrose has declared a rebellion," he said.

"Yes," the man answered dryly. "I was aware of that. I suspect almost everyone on Mars is now aware of it."

"Then what do you aim to do about it?" the Administrator demanded. "I want him stopped!"

"That did occur to me," the shield answered. "And I'm working on it. But haven't you heard that there's a citywide computer problem? We can't get our detection gear to work yet. It'll be a while before we can." He stared evenly back. "You'll have to accept that Montrose's message will be on the air a while yet. I'd suggest you prepare a countermessage, denouncing the man as a terrorist. Some people, of course, will be won over by his appeal, but they'll be badly armed and ill-trained. None of them will be able to stand up to my men."

The Administrator wanted to scream. "You're talking civil war!" he snapped. "The very thing I worked hard to prevent. We can't have any civil unrest here."

"It's too late to prevent it now," the shield informed him. "Montrose knows of our plans, and is determined to stop us. We have to win the coming battle."

"Then do it!" the Administrator yelled. "Stomp them out. Make an example of them so that nobody else even *thinks* of causing trouble."

"That's what I'm paid for," the shield answered. "I promise you, we'll do our best — just as soon as our computers come back fully on-line."

"If they're not on-line now, how can we be speaking to each other?" the Administrator demanded.

"Because the rebels deliberately left the communicators alone," the man answered. "I think they want people to talk to one another and to spread the word of the rebellion. We could shut it down ourselves if you wish."

"And then how would we talk to each other?" the Administrator asked. "Just get onto tracking down and destroying Montrose. And fast!" He turned off the communicator and collapsed backward into his chair.

How could this be happening? Montrose wasn't capable of jamming the computers like this, or of taking over the NewsNet. He had to have help. . . . And this couldn't have happened at a worse time! The Administrator had just informed Quietus that everything was ready for them to move out here. . . .

If they knew the truth, they wouldn't be giving him a hero's reception. They'd probably send him outside without a pressure suit. . . .

And death outside by explosion would be a lot better than some of the deaths that Quietus might be able to invent for him . . .

He had to get this stupid rebellion under control, fast.

12

Tristan handed over control of the hovercraft to
Barker's man — he still didn't know the thug's name,
and the man had barely spoken two sentences since
they'd met. It was probably just as well, really. He was
good at following orders without complaint, and he
could be trusted to keep the craft lined up for a return
to New York once again. Tristan went back to the passenger cabin, where things were certainly a lot noisier.

Marten and Sarai had both recovered from the effects of the riot gas, and were slouched sullenly in their
seats, their restraints preventing too much movement.
Barker and Lili sat back, watching. Mora was alone on

the other side of the cabin, watching through hooded eyes. Tristan could see that something had made her angry.

Genia, on the other hand, was being cold and aloof, striving to pretend she didn't care about her father. It was difficult to know what the girl was thinking sometimes, but Tristan was getting a little better at it. For all of her protests about being independent, he realized that she hated being alone, and she envied those of them with a normal family life.

Not that Tristan's life was normal at this time. He hadn't seen his parents for over a week now, and had no idea where they were. With a pang, he realized that he missed them. He'd been mad at them for never telling him that he was adopted, but he knew he was getting over that. They had always loved him and been good to him, and he'd barely even given them a thought. He wished he could contact them and tell them he was okay, but the shields were bound to be monitoring their Terminals, hoping he'd do just that. As for Mora, he gathered that her parents had sunk into despair because of what had happened to them, and had been left at Barker's headquarters. It was hard to imagine Mr. and Mrs. Worth like that — they had always been so cheerful and friendly. But that was before their lives had been wrecked. Tristan was just glad that

Mora's younger sister, Marka, had been sent to live with an aunt; he really liked the young girl, who had helped him when Mora tried to turn him in.

So he found it ironic that Genia was jealous of him and Mora for having a family life. She had been abandoned by Marten before she'd been born, and her mother had died when Genia was a child, forcing the youngster to fend for herself. She'd done very well, but at the expense of being a loner. She had a lot of trouble fitting in with other people.

Right now, she was attempting to prove to her father that she had never needed him. Even Tristan could see the pain in her eyes, though, as she ignored the man who had abandoned her and then tried to kill her.

Barker looked up as Tristan entered the room. "We have a small problem," Barker told him. "We need to interrogate this piece of filth, but we're out of Truzac." He gestured at Lili. "She'd like to be polite and hope he'll cooperate. She" — he gestured at Mora — "prefers the idea of torturing him for answers. Me, I think that'll get us plenty of words, but how do we know if we can trust them?"

"What about Genia?"

Barker grinned. He was making sure that Marten and Sarai could hear every word of this. "Amazingly enough, she actually agrees with Mora for once. On the condition that she's the one who gets to use the tazer."

Tristan sighed. He didn't *think* that Genia would actually do it; she was just talking to express her anger and feelings of betrayal. On the other hand, he was pretty certain that Mora would — she wanted to strike out at *anyone*, to get revenge for the pain she'd suffered. And, much as he despised Marten, Tristan couldn't bring himself to intentionally inflict pain on any human being, no matter what they had done. "Why don't we just try talking?" he asked.

"Because that slime bucket will just lie to us," Barker answered.

"I'm not so sure," Tristan said. He moved closer to Marten. "You'll talk, won't you?"

Marten looked at him, anger on his face. "Why should I talk to you?"

"Because I'm not threatening to make all of the nerves in your body go white-hot in agony." He gestured at the girls. "They are. And if you don't talk to me, you'll end up talking to them." He could see that get through to Marten; there was fear in his eyes. The man was weak, he realized. He'd planned and executed a lot of pain on others, but he'd never had to face it himself. Maybe they had an advantage here. "You know who I am, don't you?"

"Yes," Marten replied sullenly. "You're the missing third clone."

"Third?" Tristan blinked, surprised. "I thought there were only the two of us — myself and Devon."

"Oh?" Marten looked amused. "Well, your information is out of date. There are three of you."

"How can there be?" Tristan couldn't understand this. "I searched EarthNet for my DNA data, and only found Devon."

Marten sighed. "That's because the third clone isn't on Earth," he answered. "He's on Mars. I thought you were him at first, to be honest."

"Mars?" Tristan felt stunned. He had *another* clone? What was he like? Evil, like Devon . . . or more like himself? Tristan's greatest fear was that Devon's evil, like his computer skills, was genetic. If that was the case, then Tristan had that horrible flaw, too, and might yet turn bad. The thought of such a fate terrified him. "Does the third clone work for you, too?"

"That's not my concern," Marten answered. "I never talked to him. I was Devon's handler, that's all. He was my project."

"You're the one responsible for teaching that monster?" Tristan looked at the man in loathing. How could any human being do such a thing?

"He's not a monster," Marten said, annoyed. "He's a

problem, true, but that's because he turned out to be just what I had hoped for — an independent thinker, with astonishing skills." He stared at Tristan. "And, considering the fact that you've been neglected, you turned out quite like him."

"I'm *nothing* like him!" Tristan yelled.

Marten chuckled. "Scared that you are, eh? Well, you were designed to be a genius, and I'm glad to see that it worked. You shouldn't be fighting us, Tristan — you're better than the common herd, as we in Quietus are. You should be one of us, working for us, not against us."

It was one of the most sick — and *wrong* — things Tristan had ever heard, and he was about to say so when Genia pushed past him to confront her father.

"And what about me?" she asked. "I'm as clever with computers as he is. Don't you want to offer me a place in your world? Or are you still determined to kill me?"

"It's nothing personal," Marten informed her. "You were simply in the way. If you really want to join us, I'm sure you might prove useful."

"And if I didn't, then I could always be killed later?" Genia spat in his face. "Well, that's what I think of you and your offer." She whirled around and walked off a few paces — where she could still hear what was being said.

Tristan smiled slightly at the uncomfortable man. Marten couldn't wipe his face, and Genia's spit was sliding down his cheek. "I'd say pretty much the same thing," Tristan admitted. "But I think I'll skip spitting in your face. I'd prefer just seeing you *really* locked away for the rest of your life." Marten had been willing enough so far to confess to his crimes, probably because he was quite proud of himself really, and partly because he realized that they already knew most of the details. Getting fresh information out of him wouldn't be so easy, unless he thought they already knew it. The hardest part of this questioning was coming up, because Tristan was guessing on most of what he had to sound confident about. One mistake, and Marten would know it.

"Anyway, I don't think much of the efficiency of your organization," he said. "We're doing a lot better without you. After all, we haven't lost Devon, like you have."

That sparked interest in Marten's eyes, but the man tried to hide it. "You're bluffing," he said, but there was hunger in his voice. So far, Tristan had him hooked.

"You're the one they call the Malefactor, aren't you?" he asked. That was a guess, since Montoya had never named him that. But Tristan was sure he was right: Marten had admitted he was in charge of Devon, and the Malefactor had shown up when Tristan had been in

Devon's apartment in Overlook. "Who do you think you talked to in Overlook? Devon?" He shook his head and grinned. "That was me, destroying Devon's stockpile of the Doomsday Virus."

"You?" Marten was clearly shocked.

"Me," Tristan said. "You looked a lot better in that shapeless black disguise of yours. Much more imposing than you do now. Of course, being caught flat-footed doesn't help much, does it? You lost Devon, you let me go, and then you got yourself captured."

"What a big, fat zero," Genia chimed in. "A loser all around. I'll bet that Quietus *really* wants you back — so they can kill you, inch by inch, for being such a monumental failure."

That clearly hurt Marten's pride. "I'm one of their most valuable members!" he snarled. "Without me, they'd be nowhere!"

"Right," jeered Tristan. "A complete loser? What would they ever need you for?"

"The Doomsday Virus," Marten said smugly.

This was what Tristan had been after. Montoya was right — Marten *did* have a sample of the virus! Tristan had thought it had all been destroyed, but if Quietus had it . . . Luckily it didn't sound as if they had it yet. Marten wanted to keep it to prove he was indispensable. There was still a chance of destroying it. . . .

Sweat was trickling down Tristan's back, but he hoped he was keeping the fear off his face. "What good will that do you?" he mocked. "I've destroyed it before, and I can do it again. I'm smarter than Devon, and I'm *way* smarter than you. There's no way that virus can do any damage. You can't do anything with it without Devon's help, and you've lost him! You are of no use to Quietus at all."

"That's what you think," Marten growled. "I'm no slouch at computer programming myself. I used the sample I tricked you into giving me to replicate the virus. I have it stored, ready for release. I don't need Devon any longer for that. As soon as Quietus sends my Terminal the signal, it will release into EarthNet again. I don't even need to be there." He must have seen the shock and dismay in Tristan's face, because he grinned widely. "In fact, there's always a chance it may go off early. You see, I've programmed it so that if anyone but me tries to gain access to my files, the Doomsday Virus will automatically release." He shook his head. "And if I've recovered from the riot gas, so has everyone else at the prison. How long do you think it's going to be before someone starts to muck about with my setup? They may even have started it already."

Tristan went cold. Marten was obviously telling the

truth, because he had no reason to lie about it. His computer was booby-trapped. . . .

Genia saw the horror on Tristan's face and touched his arm gently. "So? That's no big deal, right? Your stealth dogs stopped the virus last time, and they can do it again."

"It's not that simple," Tristan said, numbly. "All of my stealth dogs were destroyed by the virus when they fought it. I'd have to program some more. And that would take hours. If this creep is telling the truth, we haven't *got* hours. It may already be too late."

"Not yet, it isn't," Barker said firmly. "This hovercraft is tied into EarthNet for navigation. If the Net had gone down, we'd know."

"So we have a short while, maybe," Tristan said. "I'd better get moving. I just hope we have the time for me to make the dogs." He hurried toward the cabin, where he could get onto the Terminal there and start work.

"Dream on, kid!" Marten laughed. "You'll never manage! Quietus wins, despite everything!"

Genia moved to help Tristan. "It can't be that bad," she said hopefully. "Maybe he's just bluffing to scare us."

"He's not bluffing," Tristan said with complete conviction. "He's set things up to take the whole world down with him. He's a sick little monster."

"And he's my father," Genia whispered. "I guess it's no wonder that I'm a criminal, too."

"You are what you are because of yourself," Tristan assured her. "And you've only been a crook because you were forced into it. He's a monster by his own choice." But he couldn't help thinking that his own clone, Devon, was even worse than Marten. Maybe he was destined to be evil, too. How could he offer comfort to Genia if he was going to be worse than her? "Anyway, that's not important right now. We've got to go back to Ice and stop Marten's computer from being touched." To Barker's man, he ordered: "Turn us around and take us back."

"No," Barker said from behind them. He came up and tapped the navigational array. "Look at this, Tristan. It shows that a fresh force of shields has reached Ice. We daren't go back, because they'd capture us immediately. We can't use the same trick twice to get in."

Genia looked helpless. "Now what are we going to do?" she asked. "We can't go back, and there are no stealth dogs to stop the virus this time. Has Quietus won after all?"

Tristan wished he had a reassuring reply to that. But he didn't.

13

Jill Barnes led her troops into Ice, appalled at what she was seeing. The main gate guards were down. She gestured for one of her men to check the fallen shields.

"Drugged," he reported. "Not the riot gas, either. Some sort of chemical."

"There's been a raid," Barnes realized. "Two of you stay here, on full alert. Sweep for any intruders. The rest of you, with me." She hurried toward the elevator, the rest of her squad following her, ready for anything. The ride down was not fast enough for her, but there wasn't anything she could do about the speed. Once below, the doors opened, and her team fanned out.

The inmates were all waking up. They'd obviously been felled by the riot gas when the attack had taken place. A couple of the guards were still out, stopped cold by the attackers instead of the gas. Barnes realized that it couldn't have been a Quietus attack, because when they had attacked before, they'd been shooting to kill. So who had done this — and why? She glanced at the map on her hand-comp, and headed for Chen's cell. The chances were he'd be there, or close by.

He was in the corridor, looking woozy, but recovering from the riot gas. He blinked and looked confused as Barnes reached him and helped him to a chair. "What's happened?"

"There was a raid by unknown forces," she replied. She gestured for her men to spread out and check for signs of anything or anyone missing. She bent to examine Chen herself. "We seem to have arrived too late to prevent it. How are you feeling, sir?"

"*Sir?*" he echoed. "I'm a prisoner here, Lieutenant. Didn't you know that?"

"Miss Shimoda thinks you were framed by Quietus," Barnes explained. "Are you willing to take a dose of Truzac and be questioned about your allegiances?"

"Of course." Chen looked pleased with the news.

"It's what I'd expected at my trial, and didn't get — a chance to vindicate myself."

"Montoya worked for Quietus," she informed him. "She's now in jail herself." She sprayed him with the truth drug. "Who are you loyal to — the shields or Quietus?"

"The shields," Chen said firmly.

"Welcome back, sir," Barnes said with a grin. "On the authority of the head of Security, you're released from your sentence."

"Head of Security?" Chen raised an eyebrow. "Who did they get to replace me, then?"

"Miss Shimoda." Barnes grinned wider. "I think she's hoping you'll take the job back, though. She's getting very antsy sitting in your office all day."

"Serves her right." Chen got to his feet. "Well, while I'm stuck here, let's get on with the mission. We have to find out what the raiders were after."

One of the shields hurried back. "Sir, ma'am," he called, "we've found something that we think you should see. It's in one of the prisoner's cells. The man is missing. His name's Marten Scott."

"Scott . . ." Barnes breathed. "He's Genia's father. . . ."

"Genia?" Chen scowled. "The little thief I sent here?"

"That's the one. And she escaped earlier. She must have come back to free her father." Barnes reached the empty cell and peered in. There was a shield standing by a very advanced computer system. "What is a prisoner doing with a setup like that?" she wondered.

"I don't know." Chen moved forward, and sat in the seat, studying the Terminal. "It's certainly nothing he'd be given in a place like this." He reached for the speedboard. "He must have contacts somewhere. Let's check out his files and see what we can see. . . ."

To be continued in:

2099 Book #5:

meltdown

about the author

JOHN PEEL is the author of numerous best-selling novels for young adults. There are six books in his amazing Diadem series: *Book of Names, Book of Signs, Book of Magic, Book of Thunder, Book of Earth,* and *Book of Nightmares.* He is also the author of the classic fantasy novel *The Secret of Dragonhome,* as well as installments in the Star Trek, Are You Afraid of the Dark?, and The Outer Limits series.

Mr. Peel currently lives just outside the New York Net, and will be 145 years old in the year 2099.

Discover how it all began.

STAR WARS®

JEDI APPRENTICE